THE SWAN &
THE PHOENIX

A ONCE UPON ACADEMY DUET

BIRD'S EYE VIEW & PHOENIX RISING

KERRY EVELYN

Swan Press

To my grandmother, Evelyn,
lover of swans and the best friend ever.
I miss you.

Sign up at KerryEvelyn.com to receive the password to unlock the map of Once Upon Academy and other fun extras on the Freebies tab!

PRELUDE
BIRDS OF A FEATHER

When the curtain finally fell, I released my smile and the tension began to lift. I'd done it. What they'd always wanted for me. I'd followed in my mother's footsteps and danced the part of Odette, bringing her story to life.

The adrenaline high was enough to numb the pain in my toes, but it couldn't keep my thoughts from racing. The difficulty of the part, paired with the merciless choreographer's flair and the costumer's elaborate feather overlay, demanded my full attention.

And I'd executed it flawlessly.

But was it enough? Had I projected the passion and pain my mother had felt as she danced within her tower prison for several long years? Had I captured the joy she felt when she and my father's love broke the curse and destroyed her captors?

Tonight was a big night for me. This was my last performance as a high schooler, but I'd never been to an actual high school. It was the tradition in our kingdom for royalty and nobility to be tutored in the palace under the greatest minds. After completing the rigorous courses and learning the basics of monarchy management, we'd be sent away to post-secondary schools to further our education and see the world. Some would become military officers, and others would return to support operations. Since my brother was the heir to the throne, I wasn't under that kind of pressure. Instead, I had a talent for dance and it was my mother's desire that I'd one day rise to her level of fame and land myself a prince. And the only way to do that, she thought, was through magic or academic excellence at the "right" school.

And magic was not an option available to me. My parents were human—well, at least, my father was. My mother, born a human, was cursed to live as a swan in the daytime by an evil wizard who was determined to marry her. She refused, and the wizard obliterated her kingdom —and her family. Legend has it that the beautiful lake that appeared below my father's castle around the same time was actually the tears her mother cried before she was killed.

Having spent most of her teenage years confined to swan form by day and imprisoned by night, my mother hadn't known there were prestigious schools for royalty and those with magical talents when she was my age.

Nicknamed the Swan Princess, she'd unwillingly became magical, and still has the ability to shift into a swan if she desires. Though her shapeshifting ability was born of a curse, she grew to appreciate it because it made her special and brought her attention. When it became apparent I had no such abilities to shapeshift, she'd been disappointed. As a young girl, I sensed that and was desperate to please her. I'd sneak from my bedroom to her studio to watch her dance when I was supposed to be sleeping. One day, she caught me watching and instead of being angry like I expected, she taught me the foot positions and a few basic moves.

I was a natural, and for the first time, I felt that she was proud of me. She and my father made plans for my course of study and told everyone who'd listen about their daughter's talent. When I was eleven, I began dancing with the Royal Ballet, and now, at eighteen, I was the prima ballerina they'd dreamed I'd be. There were just two pieces left to the puzzle: post-secondary school, and a prince.

I could care less right now about the prince, but secretly I wanted to go to a magical school. Years ago, a tipsy Duchess of Eagleshire had let it slip about a school that was so selective, even some who had both magical abilities and noble blood didn't get admitted. One had to have a bright mind, magical DNA, or other requirements that were never publicized. My mother, constantly trying to impress the Duchess and others like her, set her mind on my brother and I attending. He'd chosen military service, and I was her last hope. And I had no magical powers whatsoever.

That didn't deter my mother. Of course, if you ask me, her magic was more of a curse than a blessing. I didn't have any magic. People often told me that watching me dance felt like magic, but that wasn't a power. Nevertheless, my parents were confident that if anyone could get into one of those magical schools, it was their daughter.

And if I didn't, it would be just another disappointment to add to their list. I was used to that by now. Eighteen years of *if only you could do this, if only if you did this a little better, why don't you try this?*

I loved ballet, but I wasn't sure if I wanted to dance for the rest of my life. Currently, I filled my spare time teaching creative movement to preschoolers. I loved them, but it was limiting. I wanted more, but I didn't know what. I prayed that whatever school I ended up at would help me figure that out.

I also prayed to God every day that I would not turn into a swan, like my mother.

Ever.

I was afraid of birds. The wizard that cursed my mother into a swan haunted her in daylight in the form of an owl. When my brother and I were young children, she'd frighten us into obedience that there were others out there that preyed upon kids who didn't listen to their parents.

Back to the performance. After the final curtain drop

my parents pushed their way through the throngs of people to congratulate me. It was enough, they assured me. I could tell my mother was nervous. It had to be enough. It became second nature to do what I was told.

Never had they told me that I was enough. Hearing this for the first time didn't have the effect I'd expected. Instead, it made me more jittery. More pressure.

When everyone but family members and significant others of the cast left, I excused myself to go back to my dressing room and change for the reception.

One of the perks of being both the prima ballerina and the princess was having a dressing room all to myself, so I was surprised when I opened the door to find a woman standing there. Diminutive and pale-skinned with sleek onyx hair curling just above her shoulders, she shouldn't have held a commanding presence, but she did. I stood in the doorjamb, in awe of her, unsure what to say.

I could tell she was important, and when I caught sight of the scroll in her hands, I knew that was important, too. I closed the door softly behind me and stared at her, incredulous.

This was it. I'd done it.

"Antoinette." The voice was almost girly, but it was kind, in a sing-song kind of way. "I usually don't deliver these in person, I've heard so much about your dancing that I had to see it for myself." She held out the scroll.

I took it and untied the gold-edged purple ribbon. It didn't open, so I turned it over. The wax seal bore a coat of arms from *the* school, the most prestigious, the one my mother had prattled on about to me since she'd first heard about it years ago.

I carefully slid my finger under the edge of the paper and broke the seal. Unrolling it, I glanced at the woman. She nodded, and I began to read.

Dear Antoinette,

Congratulations! Once Upon Academy would be delighted if you'd consider us for your post-secondary education. With your particular talents, we believe we can best assist you in your career and life. At OUA, you'll discover your truest self and receive the finest education that will prepare you for your destiny.

The academic and personal accomplishments you have already achieved in your studies and in your community reflect the values we expect in our students. Ambition, compassion, and a curious intellect are the heart of the Once Upon Academy experience. You can be proud to have joined this select group of students.

I READ ON, and my hands began to shake. I'd done it. I'd really done it! I bit my lip. Yep, that hurt. This was real. I'd done enough. I *was* enough.

But logic crept its way into my thoughts. How was this possible? If Once Upon Academy was for the most gifted and talented, how had I earned a spot without powers?

When I finally looked up, the headmistress nodded. "You've earned your place, Nettie."

Nettie? She knew my nickname? What else did she know?

"Thank you. I never thought...My mother always hoped...I don't understand. It's mostly a school for those who have magical DNA. I can't do magic, and I hardly think my mother being cursed to turn into a swan counts."

The Headmistress giggled. "Oh, don't you worry. You haven't stepped into your true self yet, if you'll pardon my pun. You've been dancing in your mother's footsteps. And while extraordinarily talented, there's more to you than you know just yet. And we would be honored to help you cultivate your talents and navigate the coming years."

I didn't know what to say. I thanked her, and she left. I rolled up the scroll and stuffed it into my bag.

I appreciated that she'd given the letter to me privately. I'd gotten into the school, but would I fit in? Was this really best path for me? Would I make a fool of myself among a community of students far more gifted than me? How would my parents feel about that? And if it didn't work out, then what would I do?

Stewing on all these new insecurities, I changed out of my costume and into a formal white gown for the post-performance reception. After pulling out my bun and dozens of bobby-pins, I cursed the amount of hairspray that was needed to keep every strand in place, I did the best I could to finger-comb my blonde hair into some-what-presentable loose waves and toned down my makeup. Finally, I clasped my swan pendant around my neck.

Amazing how heavy a little charm could feel.

You've got this, Nettie. I took a deep breath and opened the door.

BIRD'S EYE VIEW

NETTIE'S STORY

PROLOGUE

His blood boiled. If what he saw was true, he had a brother.

Which meant his father, the King, had another son.

An older son.

The rightful heir.

A bastard brother, whom he was certain his father would claim.

Where did that leave him?

He pushed his way through the crowd of co-eds celebrating in the lake. Spirit Splash was a tradition at Once Upon Academy, one he'd been looking forward to.

Until he'd seen the mark.

The same birthmark his father had.

The same birthmark he'd never had, much to the

confusion of his family, for how could the oldest male child *not* have the mark? There was only one explanation.

He wasn't his father's oldest male child.

The mark had been passed on to someone else.

And that someone else was here, at the lake, sporting the lanyard worn by the seniors who ran the event.

When the senior turned, laughing it up with his buddies, water droplets clinging to his tanned skin, he saw it.

The resemblance, and the nametag attached to the lanyard. *Reggie.*

He'd be watching. If his suspicions were correct, Reggie's most vulnerable moment would be upon him soon.

And then he'd strike.

"Baby chickies!" Unable to contain her excitement, four-year-old Anabelle hopped and fidgeted with each syllable, all the while pulling at her pink leotard and tights. "Mommy says I can name them all after they hatch!"

"Chicks? Um..." Nettie pressed her lips together as the little girl ran in a circle around the ballet studio, arms straight out at each side to simulate flying. Nettie hated birds. Just the thought of nine little balls of downy feathers pecking at her feet made her squirm. When she'd received her acceptance letter to Once Upon Academy, she expected classes and extracurricular activities that would challenge her. She'd never dreamed of anything this...*fowl.* She almost snorted at the pun, but there was nothing funny about this predicament.

"Nine of them! They'll be so darling! But they won't be

able to fly, sweetie." The young mother intercepted the wiggly preschooler and hefted her onto her hip.

Anabelle frowned. "No flying?"

"No flying," her mother repeated.

Nettie smiled and handed Anabelle the ballet slipper she'd kicked off. "Have you already picked names?"

Anabelle's eyes lit up as she scratched at the tightly-pulled bun atop her head. "Yes, but I only have seven names."

Nettie nodded seriously. "Hm. That *is* a problem. Tell me what you have so far and maybe I can help."

Anabelle's mother gave up trying to hold her and allowed her to slide to the floor. Nettie crouched down to be eye-level with the fidgety ballerina. "Okay, but it's a secret. Just me, Mommy, and you, okay?"

Nettie bent down and nodded solemnly. "I promise not to tell *anyone*."

"Okay!" Anabelle grabbed Nettie's head by the ears and pulled it toward her face. Her lips touched Nettie's ear as she whispered loudly. "There are only seven colors in the rainbow and nine chicks. Red, orange, yellow, green, blue, indigo, violet. I need two more!"

Nettie scrunched her forehead as Anabelle jerked her head so that they were now nose to nose. "A big problem indeed. Let's see. Where can we find rainbows?"

"In the sky, silly!"

"Right!" Nettie's eyes grew wide and Anabelle mimicked her expression. "What else is in the sky?"

"Oh! Birds. And clouds. Sometimes LOTS of clouds."

"Yes, clouds, hmmm. What color are clouds?"

"White and gray and sometimes black. You know that, Miss Nettie. Ooooooh!" Anabelle squealed as she made the connection. "More colors!"

Nettie giggled and tickled the preschooler under her chin. "Yes! You are so smart!"

"Thank you thank you! Mommy, I have more names now!"

"Yes, sweetie, I heard." She adjusted the tote bag on her shoulder and stretched out her hand for Anabelle. "Slide your slipper back on or give me the other one. Then hop up so we can leave Miss Nettie for her next class."

"Okay! Bye, Miss Nettie!"

"Bye, sweet Anabelle!"

Her mother hefted her up. "Thank you, Nettie. At least say you'll think about checking in on them while we're gone? We're leaving Monday and will be gone all next week, and it'll be just our luck that they hatch while we're away."

"Um. Okay." She crossed her arms, hating to be put on the spot with Anabelle's sweet face staring her down. It was just checking on eggs, and feeding the hen, right? Maybe she could recruit Clara to help.

"Fantastic! Thank you! I'll call you tomorrow!" Anabelle's mother whirled around and was out the door in a flash. Nettie stood, there, her feet rooted in first position, dread in her gut, clenching and tugging and twisting at the thought of being that close to baby birds.

And what they might do to her.

"I can't do it, Clara."

"Of course you can," her best friend assured her. They were sitting on the bench in the ballet studio, changing out of their pointe shoes after a vigorous workout. They often stayed well after their classes ended to dance out their frustrations. Nettie had been particularly focused tonight.

"Nope." Nettie pulled on low boots and adjusted her legwarmers. "If you help me, maybe."

"I wish I could, like I said. But Hans and I have meetings all week with the Sugar Plum Fairy. We'll be in the Land of Sweets all next week after classes, remember?"

"Right. Seems strange she'd call you out of school for a whole week so early in the semester."

Clara sighed. "Well, Christmas stops for no one, and since she agreed to let us manage the Christmas Eve festivities, she needs to be sure we start planning now so that we have ample time to rehearse for the show."

Outside the Arts Building, the first signs of autumn were beginning to appear. The green was subtly yielding to rusts and reds, and the ground was littered with clumps of brown pine needles. Nettie loved the walk from the studio to their dorm room. As the sun began to set, its rays reached out over the campus, casting beams of light on the fortress and surrounding area.

Clara whistled back as a songbird swooped by them. "I know you don't like birds," she said as the bird disappeared into the open window of the headmistress's office. "I've always wondered how the daughter of a swan came to be repulsed by them."

"They're dirty, weird-looking...I just don't like them. Ugh." She shuddered and fingered the swan pendant that hung from her neck. The necklace was a gift from her mother, with a reminder not to forget her heritage. She should take it off—her mother wouldn't know. Odette hadn't a clue about Nettie's fear; showing it would admit weakness. Her parents loved her and wanted the best for her, but sometimes she felt they didn't know how to show it.

Clara shot her a pointed look. "Lame."

Nettie sighed. Someday she'd tell Clara why she didn't like birds, especially swans. But not today.

"What's lame is you ditching me on yet another Friday night for Prince Nutty," Nettie teased.

"His name is *Hans*. Oh, please, you know you'd rather be up in the Astronomy Tower stargazing than staring at a screen or going to an event."

"True." Nettie followed Clara into their room and dropped her bag on the floor. "I don't have any private lessons tomorrow, so I'm going to stay overnight at the tower. There's a meteor shower in a few hours."

"Just be careful. Those woods can be scary at night."

"Aw, you worry too much. I'll be fine as long as I stick to the protected path. Thanks, friend."

"Always!" Clara grabbed her robe and shower caddy. "Now to get prettied up for my hot date! You have fun and be careful!"

"Shouldn't I be saying that to you?" Nettie giggled. She was grateful to have a best friend like Clara. They'd known each other their whole lives thanks to their parents' love of ballet.

Eight o'clock. If she hurried, she could shower, pack snacks and essentials, and get out to the tower by 9:30.

TWO

Reggie slid down the wall outside the infirmary and rested on his haunches. He'd never felt this sick.

The attending nurse checked his vitals and insisted everything was normal. Sweating and feeling feverish were normal? In what world?

He tossed back four fever-reducers and took a sip of water. Her thermometer had to be broken. He hated having to cancel his skydiving lessons. As a fifth-year senior-slash-grad student, it was all he looked forward to. He supposed he *could* stop delaying his graduation, but then what would he do?

All he wanted to do was fly, but not in an airplane. It was too confining. He needed to feel the wind in his face, adjust the drag, and calculate the landing. It wasn't just a hobby to him.

It was everything.

But why? He had no magic, no gifts. He didn't even know who his real parents were. He and his older sister Aida had been adopted shortly after he was born. He missed her terribly; being sixteen years older, she'd been more like a mother than a sister to him. She died when he was seventeen.

He'd received his acceptance letter a week later.

The headmistress just smiled at him sweetly that day four years ago when he'd questioned the legitimacy of his letter. It wasn't a mistake, she assured him. In time, all would be revealed.

Sure, but how long was he supposed to wait? It had been *four years*.

Reggie looked up as footsteps sounded on the stone floor.

"Hey, man, you look terrible."

"Hey, Krish." The freshman had taken a few skydiving lessons with him during the first few weeks of the semester. In a way, he was glad he'd had to cancel this afternoon's lessons. Krish was the most challenging student he'd ever flown with. Stiff, afraid of heights, and heavy as lead.

Everything he wasn't.

He couldn't understand why a guy so obviously afraid of heights and flying would want to be strapped to another dude while soaring stories above the ground. Krish initially told him he was trying to overcome the fear, and if that was true, he still had a long way to go. Some people just weren't meant to fly.

Krish held out a hand to help him up. "Came looking for you when I saw you'd canceled class. You need anything?"

Reggie took his hand. "Thanks, man. Nah, just need to get some rest." Even slumped over, Reggie towered over the younger man.

Krish peered up at him as they walked. "Dude, you're in rough shape. Is it...getting close to your time?"

Reggie sniffed and slowed his shuffle to a stop. "My time?"

"You don't know?"

"Know what?"

"The mark on your back?"

His birthmark? "What about it?"

Krish knitted his eyebrows and took a full moment before responding. "It's the mark of a phoenix shifter."

Reggie rubbed at his ears and shook his head. "That's crazy, man. I'm not a shifter."

Krish shrugged. "Not yet. But I've seen that mark before."

Reggie gaped at him. "On who?"

Krish walked faster. Reggie struggled to keep pace. "Not important. But if this is what I think it is, you need to get to an isolated location for the transformation. It could be dangerous."

They exited the building. The full moon lit up the night sky. "How do you know about this?"

"Again, not important right now. There's a tower deep in the woods across the lake. You know the one, behind the Headmistress's Mansion?"

"The observation tower?"

Krish nodded. "You could go there. You'd be out of the way and couldn't hurt anyone."

Reggie's head was spinning. "Wouldn't it be better just to stay here in the infirmary? Or get Ms. Red? Or both? Surely they've seen worse and could help, if this is what you say it is."

"No!" Krish leaped in front of Reggie. "I'm sorry. But time is of the utmost importance. And from the looks of it, your transformation is already beginning. Look at your fingernails."

Reggie gasped, horrified. They'd grown long and tapered into points. His heart pounded. "How much time do I have? How long will this take?"

"I'll help you get there. From what I've heard, the first transformation can take hours, because you have to start as a hatchling and grow into a full-size bird. Then it becomes instant once you master it. We'll go there now. C'mon."

Reggie adjusted his backpack and jogged after Krish. *A phoenix shifter?*

THREE

Nettie's gaze was trained on the skylight as the air mattress inflated in the tower's circular observation room. The full moon was bright and lit up the surrounding clouds. If they didn't dissipate, it would be hard to see the meteor shower.

She spread her sleeping bag over the mattress and crawled inside the warm, insulated faux-down sack. *Alarm set. Eyes closed.*

Chicks. Chick-sitting. Chick-tastic. She was never getting to sleep if all she could think about and see behind her eyelids were birds.

She hated birds, and birds hated her.

Otherwise, that swan wouldn't have tried to eat her.

It was an honest mistake. When you're three and you've been told your mother can change into a swan, it's natural to assume that a lone swan on your favorite pond is your mother swimming around. Wasn't it?

How was she supposed to know it wasn't her mother and it didn't like giving rides to little girls?

Nettie shuddered at the memory. Well, that was all in the past. She was a grown-up now, a college freshman. Not a scared preschooler. Even her four-year-old students weren't scared of birds.

It was ridiculous, really. Saying no to an easy job because she was afraid of a hen and some baby chicks?

She unhooked her necklace and slid it into a small zippered compartment in her backpack. It seemed Nettie was always surrounded by birds, no matter where she went or how much effort she put into avoiding them. Tonight, she'd be bird-free.

Deep, male voices in the stairwell carried up and through the space under the heavy cement door. Nettie froze. Did she remember to lock it? She hadn't considered anyone else showing up to watch the meteor shower. It was Friday night, and the Astronomy Tower was so far off the beaten path, it wasn't even on the campus map. Everyone had something better to do, she was sure.

Evidently not everyone.

She pulled herself to a sitting position as the door opened next to her. She braced herself, but it didn't swing wide enough to crush her. A man's hand gripped the side of the door.

"Thanks for helping me get out here, Krish."

Nettie sucked in a breath as she recognized the TA from her mythology class.

Reggie.

Holy hotness. She'd been crushing on him since the first class. This week, she'd finally mustered the confidence to sit up front. Mythology fired him up. She had to admit, she'd been dreading the class. Instead, she was hanging on to every word and racking her brain for something clever to say to get his attention.

Nettie drew up her knees and pushed her back into the wall. The voices were louder now.

"What do you mean you're leaving? You told me an hour ago I couldn't get through this by myself?" It was a question, not a statement. What was Reggie talking about? What did he have to get through, and why did he have to do it here?

"I just need to run back to the dorm," Krish said smoothly, with an edge of nonchalance to spark Nettie's suspicion. "I forgot—something."

Reggie took a step back, hand still gripping the door, but now in Nettie's line of sight. The full moon cast a beam through the open window where he was standing, slightly bent over. She couldn't see all of him, just the back of his head, shoulders, a lumpy backpack, the roundness of his backside.

Chill, Nettie. You've got more important things to focus on, like this kink in your plan. Were they planning to watch the meteor shower? If Krish was leaving to head back to the dormitories, she'd have about an hour alone with Reggie before Krish returned. What would she say? What would they talk about? Would she even be able to speak, or would her painful shyness keep her silent?

Reggie said goodbye and closed the door. *Say something, Nettie!*

She coughed.

Reggie jumped and whirled in her direction. He pulled his phone out and swiped. As his flashlight caught her in its path, she squinted. A slow grin formed on his lips. "Hey." He dimmed the light and pointed it away from her. "Sorry."

Nettie pressed her lips together and held her hand up in a wave.

His eyes scanned her setup. "Camping out?"

"Um." Her eyes darted to the window. "There's a meteor shower in a couple hours."

"Right. I knew about that. You're in my class. Antoinette, right?"

A fizzy sensation bubbled in her gut and up her center. He knew her name? "Nettie." She held out her hand and immediately regretted it. *Dork! You already know each other!*

Reggie slid his backpack off his shoulder and tossed it on the floor and shook her hand. His fingernails scraped her wrist. *Odd.*

"Nice to meet you officially, Nettie. Sorry to disturb

your night…May I sit?" He gestured to the end of her air mattress.

Nettie pulled her feet toward her and wrapped her arms around her knees. "Sure."

He mimicked her position and leaned back against the wall just down from her. Closing his eyes, he took a ragged breath. He shook slightly, as if he was cold.

"You okay?" Nettie asked.

His eyes popped open. "I—don't think so," he muttered. Letting out a long sigh, he let his shoulders slump. In the semi-darkness, it was hard to see his face clearly, but she sensed something was off.

"Reggie?"

He closed his eyes as a serious of wheezy coughs made him pause. "You shouldn't be here."

"Why not? Are you okay?" She looked up. Above, the stars twinkled through the glass. "There's plenty of space for the three of us to watch the event."

Reggie smiled, but didn't open his eyes or turn to look at her. "I'm not here for that. I forgot all about it actually."

Nettie shifted her body to face him. In the dim light, it was hard to tell just how sick he might be. "So then you came here to avoid infecting the student body with your magical illness?"

Reggie met her gaze, eyes glowing slightly. She definitely did not misread the anguish in his expression. "It's too incredible to believe."

"Really? We attend a secret school for kids with magical talents," Nettie stated dryly. "Try me."

"Point taken." His voice was getting hoarser. "If what Krish tells me is true, I'll be shifting into a phoenix at some point in the next twelve hours."

Nettie recoiled. Of course it had to be a bird! She had to get out of there. Crush or no crush, she was not sticking around for that. A phoenix was a *big* bird, a *flamey* bird. The baby chicks were starting to sound almost cute in comparison.

Speak calmly. "I believe you. My mother shifts into a swan. No problem. I can go somewhere else." She slid out of the sleeping bag and stood up to fold it.

"Thanks." Reggie took her outstretched hand and she pulled him up.

Wow, he was really struggling. Perspiration beaded his forehead and his face had taken on a graying pallor. She rubbed at the scratches on her wrists. "I think I'll wait 'til Krish gets back to leave."

He nodded and slid down the wall. She kept an eye on him as she deflated the air mattress and rolled it up. In a few minutes, all her belongings were rolled and packed.

"Is there anything I can do?" she asked. His wavy, styled black hair was beginning to droop with moisture. She tentatively put her hand on his upper back. Soaking wet and burning up.

Something thumped on the other side of the door.

Reggie pressed his hands on the floor and struggled to a standing position. He waved Nettie off. "I got this."

He stumbled to the door. Nettie worried he was deteriorating too fast. She'd never seen her mother shift. Was this what it was like for her, too? For the first time, she wished her fear hadn't kept her from learning more about her mother's shapeshifting capabilities. She'd never thought much about them, or the process of shifting.

Reggie pulled at the handle on the door. "Door's stuck, Krish."

"No, it's not." The voice on the other side was calm, confident. Nettie joined Reggie at the door and they tugged together. Definitely stuck. She shrugged.

"Krish, can you push?" Reggie asked.

Another thump. Nettie and Reggie exchanged a glance and gave another tug.

"Krish? Can you hear me?"

Silence.

"Krish?" Reggie's voice was barely audible, and the next tug set him into a coughing fit. Hunched over, he tried to speak. "I can't open the door."

"You're on your own, brother!" Krish's voice had an ominous edge to it. "The barricade is charmed into place."

"Brother?" He leaned on Nettie for support. "What...do you...mean?"

"Your mark. My whole life, they wondered why I didn't have it. I, the eldest son of the king. I saw you at the lake. You could be his younger brother the way you resemble him so closely. The mark confirmed it. My father still pines for his long-lost love who disappeared without a trace. He's never been able to love my mother the way he loved her, and I'll not have you replace me!"

"But...I'll die...I don't know what to do. You said I needed someone by my side or I'll become a pile of dust."

"Exactly. Goodbye, brother."

S on of a king? It couldn't be true.

He leaned on Nettie as she eased him back to the wall. When he was settled, she went back to the door and tugged on it.

"It's definitely stuck shut," she said. "He must have barricaded it from the other side."

"But...it opens...inward." Reggie's head was spinning. None of this was making any sense.

"Maybe I can—"

"No." Reggie shook his head. "It's too dangerous. He said there'll be fire, and I'll be wild, and—"

He studied her face. Genuine concern, sheer panic, and utter determination warred in her eyes. Her pale cheeks flushed with color. She looked...warm. He was freezing.

"Well, I'm not going anywhere unless I jump out that

window. Though tempted, I doubt I'd survive the fall, which makes me a helper by default."

"He doesn't know...you're here."

"Which is just what you need to have a chance to survive this." Nettie began unpacking her bag. "You're shivering and burning up at the same time. I'll set up the air mattress again, and you'll get in my sleeping bag and try to warm up."

"Bossy." Reggie gave a weak smile and toed off his sneakers.

She softened her tone. "We should be prepared. For right now, you're still human. The least I can do is help you get comfortable."

"I...owe you...big time."

"Nah."

It was hard to see in the dim light, but he could have sworn she was blushing. With her messy blonde hair and snow-white skin, Nettie was stunning. Like an ice princess. But warm.

Warm. He was shaking violently now, and she was looking at him oddly.

"Um." Nettie pressed her lips together and felt the back of his forehead with her hand. "I have a suggestion, but—"

"But?"

Nettie dropped her hand as if scalded. "You look like you're freezing, but your temp is high. I can—" She sucked in a deep breath and let it back out, squeezing her eyes shut. "I can...get in there, with you." Her eyes opened wide. "Or not. Up to you." She spoke the last two sentences fast.

It was charming how uncomfortable she was with her offer. His heart tugged, and he nodded. "Please. C'mere."

She scooted up next to him but didn't make a move to get in the sleeping bag. Their eyes met. "Should I, um—"

"If you...unzip it..." He struggled to be audible. His throat was on fire. "We can—blanket—both—"

"Yes." Nettie unzipped the bag and helped rearranged it over him. "I'm sorry I don't have a pillow for you."

Reggie scooched over toward the wall to make room for her on the mattress. "This...is... a hundred times... better than...the cold stone."

"Shh, don't talk. Save your strength for the trans-formation."

He lifted his arm and she turned on her side, resting her head in the space between his arm and collar bone. "So much...better. Thank you...If I start to burn, please... just...leave me."

"I'm not leaving you." Nettie turned on her side and wrapped an arm around his chest. "Is this okay?" she whispered. The moonlight shone on her face. In the soft glow of light, she could have been an angel.

No, she was an angel. His angel. He could even picture her with a pair of white feathery wings. Appearing out of nowhere and offering to help a virtual stranger survive something that could kill them both.

N ettie chattered on about everything and nothing until Reggie fell asleep. To keep him distracted, she told him about her parents, her dancing, her struggle to figure out what she was supposed to do with her life. She worried she'd gotten too personal. Talking to Reggie was so easy, and he fretted less while she was droning on. She had every reason to believe her mother's transformations were easy, seamless. Not like this.

He burned hotter and hotter. It felt like the whole room was heating up. Nettie had removed her hoodie and t-shirt and was still sweating in her camisole. She slipped out from under the blanket and walked to the window.

She regretted never asking her mother about her shifting. It had never crossed her mind it might be dangerous, or painful, or life-threatening.

And now she was trapped in a tower. *How cliché.*

Wiping her brow, she inspected the multi-paned casement window. There had to be a latch somewhere on the old lattice panels. There it was! The panel swung out and the cool night air kissed her damp skin. Maybe she could get a cell signal if she stuck her phone out the window.

No network.

Well, first things first. Stay calm. Help Reggie survive his transformation, then figure out how to get out of the tower. She leaned on the stone sill and looked down. *Definitely not jumping or climbing out of here.* Too bad *she* wasn't a shapeshifting swan; she could fly them out.

That was it! After he transformed, she could grab on like that old professor did in that wizarding movie and *voilà!* Sure, the idea of even getting close to a bird—let alone a phoenix—was terrifying, but she could teach herself to swallow that fear real fast if doing so meant she could escape the tower. Then she'd track down that Krish kid and give him a swift *grand battement* to the throat!

What a murderous jerk. If he *was* Reggie's brother, she couldn't imagine what was going to come out of *that* Pandora's box.

"Nettie?"

"Right here." In a few strides, she was back at his side. His face glowed like it was lit up from the inside. Nettie struggled to keep her face neutral, but she was horrified.

Reggie's eyes were closed. "Can you...help me...onto the floor?"

"The floor? Why?"

"Cooler. Feeling...the heat...now."

Nettie moved behind him and slid her arms under his, clasping her hands over his chest. He had to be well over one hundred degrees. His handsome face contorted in pain and discomfort. Her chest ached, and it wasn't from the strain of hefting him to the floor.

"Thanks. Clothes?"

"Clothes?"

"Off. Please."

Oh, good Lord.

Wordlessly, she gently removed his sneakers and peeled off his socks. His feet scorched her. In the semi-darkness, the glow from within was unmistakable.

"Pants. Snaps."

Huh?

She went around to his side and lifted his hoodie and tee shirt. No snaps at his waistband, only scorching-hot, toned, glowing...*Stop it, Nettie, the man might die! If he doesn't, then you can think about...other things.*

"Sides."

Right! She pulled at the snaps that ran the length of his legs and went around to the other side to unfasten the rest. Pulling them off, she kept her eyes trained on his face, lest she be tempted to inspect what she knew would be mighty fine legs indeed. Next, she unzipped his hoodie. He was too weak to sit up, so she did her best pulling and tugging to get it and the t-shirt underneath off.

And there he was. Lying on the stone-cold floor in boxer shorts, glowing from the inside. Reggie was literally the hottest guy she'd ever met.

"Nettie." The whisper was more of a low whistle, like a teakettle when it reaches boiling. She knelt by his side and took his hands. Their heat seared her palms, but she had to ignore the pain. She'd hold on as long as she could.

SIX

Reggie was burning up. Flames licked his insides. He couldn't move. Could hardly breathe. He struggled to open his eyes, just to see her. If he was dying, he wanted her face to be the last thing he saw and thought about, not the back of his eyelids and the scorch of the fire that burned within him.

Or the fact that he had a brother, and probably a whole family out there. Krish said his father was a king. Of what? Where? Reggie and his sister had been taken in by the Almasts when he was a newborn. Unable to have children of their own, they adopted the pair and doted on them. They'd grieved his sister Aida's death as deeply as he had.

When his Academy letter arrived, none of them knew what it meant. His parents thought it was a scam until the headmistress arrived to explain after not hearing back. But she'd never alluded to him having a royal lineage or shapeshifting capabilities. Had she known? And if so, why wouldn't she have helped him to prepare?

What a day that was. Learning the storybook characters from their childhoods existed and were living their happily-ever-afters was a hard sell, but the headmistress had convinced them that she spoke the truth, and a few months later, Reggie arrived at Once Upon Academy excited and ready to find out what his gift was.

He'd waited his whole undergrad for a reveal like this, but he didn't know anything about shifting. All he knew was what Krish had told him on the way to the tower. Why couldn't he have had the power to read minds or fly or project images? What was the use of being a phoenix?

No wonder he'd always loved to fly. He was part bird.

Nettie was afraid of birds. While she was murmuring to him to lull him to sleep, she had told him her story and about the chick-sitting job offer. If he survived this, he would help her take care of the baby birds. Heck, maybe he'd even be able to talk to them. Who knew?

Krish knew. *His brother.* The moment he heard it he'd known it was true. Like a wave, it overtook him and consumed him. If the king was Krish's father, though, what of his missing birth mother? Had she died? And how did his sister figure in?

He needed to survive this and find out the whole story.

"Reggie!" Nettie's lips were on his, and she was

breathing into him. Had he stopped breathing on his own? The heat was warping his sense of reality.

Sweet girl. She was trying to resuscitate him. Maybe he *was* dying. Too bad. He wished it didn't have to end like this.

Reggie's mind went back to two days ago. He'd noticed her in the front row, smiling at him, hanging on to his every word. He'd needed to know her name. After class, he searched the roll for the initials "AC" which were monogrammed on the backpack at her feet. She was either Antoinette Chaikova or Alexis Chon. Alexis was his friend's sister, so that left just the one. In class today, he'd stolen glances when she wasn't looking. He had to play it cool; it was frowned upon for TAs to crush on undergrads, even if he was technically an undergrad himself.

Cool. He would have laughed at the irony if his internal organs were working.

Nettie. He couldn't speak. His eyes wouldn't open. Burning heat licked every fiber of his being. The last he heard was her scream as he burst into flames.

FROM ACROSS THE LAKE, Krish watched the fiery glow from the tower. So that was it, then. Under his relief, he mourned for a brother he'd never know. But it was for the best. For him, yes, but also for his parents. Their marriage would surely dissolve if his father were to find out that woman had a child—a son!—and may still be out there.

He wished he'd asked Reggie about his mother. If there was another loose end to tie up, he'd better do it quick.

But not before he returned to the tower to clean up the ashes. But that could wait until tomorrow. He checked his phone. If he hurried, he could still make it to Cindy's party.

"No-no-no-no-no!" Nettie leapt back from the flames and wept as Reggie's beautiful body burned and sparked before her eyes. She pressed against the cool tower wall, helpless.

And stuck.

She was trapped in the tower with a burning body.

Think, Nettie.

She couldn't. She didn't want to.

The fire gave way to a pile of ashes. *Oh, Reggie.* She scooted over to the piles and knelt beside where his head lay just a short time ago. Nothing remained of the handsome man she was sure she'd fallen in love with at first sight.

Her stomach wretched, and a fresh series of sobs wracked her body. She pitched forward, landing on her forearms in his ashes. She cried harder, her tears sliding off her cheeks and onto the dust.

Nettie stayed in that position for some time, until she realized the grains under her arm were moving. *What?*

She brushed the ashes off her arms and torso and sat back on her heels. The dust *was* moving. The ash on her arms detached and floated toward the pile. Particles collected and danced. Rubbing her eyes, she watched, fascinated, as he transformed before her. The piles of ash swirled together and began to take shape.

Nettie's breath caught as she realized she was witnessing a birth of epic implications.

Reggie had survived.

In front of her stood a large, featherless baby bird. *"Reggie,"* she whispered.

It turned to her and took an awkward step. She searched the bird's eyes and grinned. It was him!

Nettie held out her hand tentatively and the bird nuzzled its cheek against it. "Hey, there li'l guy."

The baby phoenix cooed, and Nettie smiled. For the first time in her life, she wasn't afraid of a bird. Heck, if she could get through this, those chicks would be a piece of cake.

The bird looked up, and Nettie followed suit. Through the glass dome, the flashes from the meteor shower sparkled.

When she next looked at Reggie, he was growing feathers. Soft down covered his head, and longer feathers of red and gold-covered his body, tail, and wings. He was transforming and growing before her eyes.

Nettie's awe morphed into laughter and finally admiration. He'd gone from looking like a plucked chicken to a gorgeous full-size phoenix in minutes. Plumes on his head and a tail flittered in the breeze from the open window.

"You should try to fly." He turned his head to her, eyes wide, and darted a glance to the window. "Here, I'll help you get up there." Nettie laced her fingers together and the bird stepped on to her palms. She was sure after all they'd been through together, he'd never hurt her. Feeling confident enough to take him into her arms, she carried him to the window sill. "I don't know how much bigger you're going to get, but it sure looks like you have all your feathers. You should try to fly."

The phoenix stretched its neck toward Nettie and rubbed its head on her chin.

"Don't worry about me. Go on."

The phoenix shook his head, looking past her toward the barricaded door.

"You can do it. Reggie. You love flying. You talk about it every class. I'll get out of here somehow."

With one last nuzzle against her hand, the bird nodded, turned to face the open window, and jumped.

EIGHT

R eggie was falling.

No, he was flying. And it was glorious.

Wow.

He'd survived his transformation, and now he was flying.

It only took a few seconds to figure out the rhythm. He climbed up, up, up, higher and higher. In his mind, he didn't feel any different—just free.

So free.

Nettie saved him. Somehow, she'd saved him.

He could feel his body growing still. He should get back and start trying to figure out how to become human again. Could he do it with his mind?

Reggie changed his course and glided down towards the tower window. He perched on the stone and watched Nettie. She sat on her air mattress, legs crossed in front of her. She was rubbing her temples. He wanted to know what she was thinking.

He opened his mouth to speak, forgetting he couldn't. A squeaky cooing sound escaped from his beak. Ooh. He'd have to work on that. It sounded wretched.

It got her attention, though. He hopped down to the floor and pranced over to her. She stroked his head.

"I don't know for sure if you can understand me. Can you?"

He nodded.

Nettie smiled. "I'm glad. Do you know how to shift back?"

Reggie shook his head from side to side. Not yet. But he was going to try. Closing his eyes, he imagined himself human again.

Concentrate. I am human.

Nothing,

Reggie closed his eyes and pictured his human self.

Still nothing.

He imagined the process. Wings to arms, feathers jutting out of his skin. His nose forming into a beak...

Nettie gasped. He opened his eyes. It was happening!

His body stretched and pulled and shook and before he could process it all, he was standing before her in his human form.

Naked.

Oops. He'd forgotten his boxers burned in the fire.

She grinned and tossed him his nylon track pants. *Bless*

you for snapping them back together. He quickly stepped into them and shot her a wink.

Nettie blushed. "It's good to see you back in your fine form. All of you," she joked. Reggie appreciated her attempt at humor. She closed the distance between them and reached a hand up to tuck his hair behind his ear. Her lips trembled. She cupped his cheek in her palm. "That was the scariest thing I've ever seen. I'm so glad you're okay." Her voice cracked.

Reggie pulled her to him, so that her ear pressed against his heart. "You hear that? My heart is beating because you saved me. I was scared, too. But you stayed with me. You cried for me. The last thing I saw before I woke up was you. Your tears cooled the heat and started the magic. Nettie, I—"

She wrapped her arms around him and squeezed. "I don't know what to say. I just know I don't want to let go."

"Then don't. Let's watch the sky, get some sleep, and figure out what's next in the morning." He guided her back to the mattress, where they assumed their original positions. Only this time, it wasn't awkward at all. As the stars reigned in the heavens, Reggie held on to Nettie.

He didn't want to let go, either.

CHAPTER
NINE

It had to be a dream.

Hadn't it?

Nettie didn't want to open her eyes. If she did, that would mean the dream was over. And though parts of it were terrifying and gut-wrenching, she was currently in the blissful part.

If she opened her eyes, everything would change. There was still the matter of Krish and his claim that Reggie was heir apparent to a kingdom. Nettie's mind raced, and anger snaked its tendrils inside of her as it occurred to her that Krish had meant for Reggie to die.

"Hey."

She turned her head. "Hey."

"You look really mad. What are you thinking about?"

She spoke tightly. "Aren't you angry? Krish tried to—"

Reggie tugged her close and flicked his chin upward.

"The sky is beautiful. To look at, to fly in. To *fly*, Nettie. Really fly. I'm not limited anymore. Don't waste a minute thinking about Krish. I'm not. I refuse to let negativity ruin the good that came out of it. I pity him, really, that he'll never experience what I will. Pretend for a moment, it's just us, here."

"But—you're a *bird*. And you could have died! He—"

He silenced her with a kiss. Sparks shot through her entire body, warming her from the inside out. Nettie closed her eyes and tried to forget about everything but how she felt right now.

Reggie had survived, and the passion behind this kiss was evidence he'd regained his strength.

She, however, had never felt so weak.

He pulled away. "Um...Nettie, I think something's happening. Your lips—"

Nettie's fingers flew to her mouth. Her lips had hardened and were growing, protruding outward. *Oh my God.* She jumped back, away from him, terrified.

Reggie stared at her. "Your mother is a swan shifter, right?"

She could only nod as her neck stretched and her legs shrunk. Nettie stared at her feet as her toes strained at her socks, webbing into flippers. Under her clothes, feathers sprouted from her skin and strained at the fabric.

This was definitely a nightmare. The blissful part had transitioned into a horror she couldn't have imagined.

Nettie was vaguely aware of Reggie removing her

clothes. She'd never pictured her first time getting naked with a guy would happen like this.

But she wasn't naked. She was covered in shimmering snow-white feathers.

Her worst fear had come true. In front of her crush, no less. A sob choked its way up her throat, emitting a sound similar to the horn on her childhood bike.

Nettie's eyes filled with tears for the second time in just a few hours. Reggie might be thrilled to be a bird, but she wasn't. She let her head droop, unable to look at him.

"Wow," Reggie reached out and stroked her head. She nuzzled into his palm. "You're the most beautiful swan I've ever seen."

She wanted to laugh. He sounded so serious. This was insane. Why wasn't he freaking out?

Nettie waddled over to the sleeping bag. Using her beak, she lifted it and pushed herself under. There had to be a way for her to shift back. Maybe if she closed her eyes and concentrated, she could will it to happen. The blanket would shield her so she wouldn't be caught naked when she shifted back.

REGGIE WATCHED the lump under the blanket with adoring curiosity. She'd figure it out, just like he had. What a pair they made.

"Take your time, Nettie. Think about becoming human again, what that takes," he advised her. "You've got this."

The blanket shifted, and an ivory foot poked out from beneath it. Nettie's blonde hair appeared at the other end, then her hand, smoothing the blanket over her. Her cheeks flushed crimson, and he suppressed a smile at her adorable distress.

"Well," he said, eyes darting to the window. "At least we know how we're getting out of the tower now."

Lips pressed together, she didn't respond to his attempt at humor. Her gaze fell to her clothes, on the floor and out of reach. He brought them to her and turned his back while she dressed under the blanket.

"You can turn back around now."

Reggie closed the distance between them and took her hands in his. He pressed his lips to her forehead. Above, the stars seemed brighter. "Are you okay?"

She leaned into him. "I am. I think. I was scared of this for eighteen years and now…I'm incredibly surprised and a bit shaken, but otherwise okay. I'm glad we could be here for each other."

"Me too. So how do you think—"

"I don't know. It was the kiss that seemed to trigger it. I wonder, maybe the owl kissed my mother?"

Reggie wasn't that familiar with the story. "So, to kick off your shapeshifting you had to be kissed by a bird?"

"I guess so." Her face fell. "My mother never wanted anything to do with that owl. He was her tormentor. To think he coerced her—magically or otherwise—into kissing him..." Nettie chewed on her bottom lip, then leaned against Reggie's body. "Let's just say I'm glad our kiss happened the way it did."

Not sure what else to say in such a heavy moment, Reggie settled for kissing the top of her head and running a hand over her hair. Then Nettie chuckled, which snow-balled into full belly laughter. "What's so funny?"

"It's just, I mean, to think me, of all people—" Nettie interrupted herself with another giggle. "I kissed a bird, and I liked it!"

Nettie leaned over the window ledge and let go of her air mattress. Down, down, down, it hugged the stone tower wall until it came to a stop in a clump of bushes. She repeated the action with her sleeping bag and backpack, and then with Reggie's backpack.

"That was somewhat satisfying." She stared at the pile of belongings several stories down, spotlighted by the waning moonlight.

Reggie laid his hand on her shoulder. "Are you ready? After I kiss you, I'll turn around so you'll have privacy."

"Thanks." They'd stripped down to their underwear so they'd have their clothes to walk back to campus. *Just like a bathing suit. Nothing he hasn't seen before every year at Spirit Splash. Look at him. Sweet guy is doing everything he can to look at my eyes.* Her heart warmed, and she nodded. "Ready."

He put his hands on her waist and she snaked hers around his neck. For this second, she was all human, and relished the current of excitement that raced through every part of her being. This kiss was passionate, full of meaning and promise.

Nettie's heart soared with hope this time. Reggie told her she'd love flying, made it sound like the most glorious thing a person could do. She was actually looking forward to this transformation.

As it started, Reggie stepped back and turned around. She quickly shed her underclothes before her wings fully formed. A swan wearing underwear and a bra would be conspicuous and ridiculous.

Nettie spread her arms as they developed into wings. Afraid or not, she was a bird. The only way to get through it was to accept it and try to enjoy it. And who better to be a bird with than a phoenix, who gave an entirely new meaning to the word "hot?"

Fully transformed, she waddled over to Reggie and nudged his backside with her beak. He crouched down and grinned. "Your turn to turn around."

She complied, and a moment later, they faced each other, bird to bird. Nettie honked in laughter when she caught sight of the undergarments next to them. What people will think when they were found in the tower, ha! She didn't care.

Reggie lifted off the ground and flew to the sill. Nettie waddled over, and after two ungraceful tries, found purchase next to him.

He took off in a flurry of red and gold feathers, circling high in the air and gliding back around to hover several feet from her. *Here goes.*

Nettie closed her eyes, spread her wings, and jumped.

She was falling. *Just jump,* he'd said. *Your instincts will kick in*, he'd promised—oh! Yes, it was happening! Opening her eyes, she relaxed as her wings guided her to the ground. This *was* fun! Kinda.

It really wasn't as bad as she'd always imagined. She'd let herself get worked up because of her fears. This flight was brief, but it was enough to feel empowered. The view from above, the tricks she could learn...She could definitely get used to flying, and having Reggie as her flight buddy would be a romantic side-bonus.

The phoenix's eyes shone with delight. He lifted off the ground and flew to the other side of the bushes. A few seconds later, Reggie appeared behind the bush from the chest up. "Can you nudge my bag closer?"

Nettie closed her beak around the strap and dragged it to him.

"Thanks." He dressed quickly. "Want me to pull out your clothes for you?"

She honked and nodded her head. The sound still surprised her. She wasn't sure she'd get used to *that* any time soon. But flying? It didn't seem so bad, especially not with Reggie by her side.

NETTIE LEANED into Reggie as they watched the sun rise over the lake and reflected on the past few hours. Her hand closed around the swan pendant at her throat, proud of her heritage and new ability.

"You ready?" She asked Reggie as her phone buzzed. They'd laid out a plan to confront Krish.

He nodded and flicked his chin toward a nearby tree. "Don't forget to grab my clothes."

She smiled slyly. "I won't forget." She looked up at him. "You may have to earn them back, though."

"Oh really?" He turned her to face him and wrapped his arms around her waist. "Is that a threat or a promise?"

"Hmm...we'll see." She rose up on her toes to press her lips to his. They'd spent an hour working on this particular skill. She had to make sure she didn't shift every time they kissed. After the third attempt, she'd been able to concentrate on him and retain her human form.

He pulled away. "See you soon." Jogging off toward the designated tree, he tossed her a saucy grin. When he soared above in his phoenix form, she collected his clothes and stuffed them into his backpack. Loaded down with all of their stuff, she headed for Krish's dorm. According to her sources, he was now stumbling back from Cindy's party.

Nettie caught sight of Krish as he rounded the corner toward the hall's entrance.

"Krish!"

Nettie gasped when he looked up. His face was an unnaturally gray pallor, and his eyes were bloodshot, as if he'd been up all night. Was he remorseful? She'd never seen anyone look so miserable.

Except for Reggie, last night.

"Do I know you?" he asked, his voice strained and gravelly.

She tossed Reggie's backpack to the ground between them. "I was in the tower last night."

His eyes widened briefly and then flashed with defiance. "I don't know what you're talking about."

"You tried to kill Reggie! Why would you do something like that?"

"I—"

"Save the lies. What do you know that made Reggie a threat?"

Krish bolted for the door of the dorm, only to be blocked by the headmistress. She exited, forcing him to retreat toward Nettie. "Ah ah aah..." she chided him.

Nettie caught Krish's eyes as he looked for an escape route. "Look up, Krish."

Above them, the majestically royal phoenix soared, its feathers catching the brilliant light of the sun.

Krish tensed. "Is that—? Reggie? How is that possible?"

"Ha! So you did try to kill him?"

"I—"

"Look at him!" Nettie's eyes followed the phoenix. Reggie showed off, executing complicated aerials and showy tricks. He was a natural. Her heart fluttered and she grinned, despite her anger toward Reggie's newly-revealed brother.

The headmistress's singsong voice brought her back. "You'd better tell the truth, Krish." Her tone was kind, but firm. "Otherwise, Ms. Fay has this wonderful Pinocchio spell she can use on you."

"Uh, well..." His shoulders sagged. "I panicked when an opportunity presented itself to save the future that I planned for. I didn't know what this would mean for me, finding a brother and all."

Nettie's temper flared. "You should have been grateful to gain a brother! What's wrong with you?"

Krish explained about his father's love affair with the mystery woman who disappeared years before his own birth. "So I figured out that Reggie had to be her son, and I thought getting rid of him would solve all my problems. But later, after I was sure he was done for, I wished I hadn't."

"Hm." The headmistress pursed her lips. "Attempted murder is a serious thing, young man. I'm going to have to call your parents. You'll be referred to Ms. Fay for your punishment."

The phoenix soared to the ground and faced Krish. Reggie's eyes flashed.

"I'm sorry, brother." Krish's shoulders sagged, and his handsome face contorted as he struggled to keep his composure.

Nettie could tell that he felt remorse; it was the only thing preventing her from kicking Krish in the face.

"Well, then, let's go to my office and figure this out." A glowing rope appeared in the air and coiled around Krish's wrists. The headmistress nodded at Nettie and Reggie as she led Krish away.

Reggie rubbed his head against Nettie's leg. She bent to stroke his silky feathers. "It'll all work out," she promised. "Let's go get you dressed and see about that flying lesson you promised me, and then I'll teach you everything you need to know about being royal."

PHOENIX RISING

REGGIE'S STORY

PROLOGUE

Ardu Almaar Palace
Early December

K rish sat stiffly in the velvet-cushioned gilded chair. If only he could reach for Saraya's hand but the ceremonial protocol forbade public displays of affection.

In front of them, the brother he hadn't known existed until recently faced the crowd of thousands as he was installed as Ardu Almaar's new Crown Prince. For the millionth time, Krish wished he'd never laid eyes on the familial birthmark on Reggie's shoulder blade. He wished he hadn't attended the Spirit Splash welcome party at Once Upon Academy.

He wished he'd never heard of Once Upon Academy.

If it hadn't been for him, no one would know the king

had an older son. Despite his illegitimate status, Reggie had been the one to inherit his father's legacy.

Now, there were consequences. Beyond the obvious—Krish was disappointed he wouldn't be king—but the worst of it would be losing Saraya.

It didn't matter that she'd lived in the palace since she was six and they'd grown up together and trained to rule together. It didn't matter that they owned each other's hearts. It didn't matter that Reggie was in love with someone else and was loved by her in return.

All that mattered was *duty*.

Saraya's duty as the Princess of Pundarika was to marry the heir to the Ardu Almaar throne.

And as of today, that wasn't Krish.

R eggie stared into the crowd, his jaw set firm like the stone walls of the palace behind him. On the morning of his installation as heir to the throne of Ardu Almaar, his heart raced with trepidation, and ached with dread and regret. He fought the urge to wipe his palms on the heavy velvet robe draped on his shoulders. The occasion should have been joyous for the long-lost crown prince, but the king had dropped an expectation on him just prior to the start of the ceremony that had him in knots.

Despite the circumstances leading up to his investiture, Reggie thought things had been going well for someone who'd recently learned his entire past had been a fairytale of a different sort than the type his classmates at Once Upon Academy lived. He finally knew where he was from. His "sister" had really been his mother, and once he digested that nugget of information, processing the idea that he was next in line to rule the tiny Eastern European country was like someone telling him fire was hot.

His birth family, save his stepmother and brother Krish, had welcomed him with open arms. Krish was four years his junior, and they were both students at the selective Once Upon Academy. Three sisters and a brother followed, the youngest of whom just turned five.

His father's reaction when he walked into the Headmistress's office to meet Reggie for the first time was a moment he'd never forget. They'd wept together, and the king had told him about his one true love, Aida, Reggie's mother, who'd disappeared without a trace six months before Reggie's birth. The king hadn't known of Reggie's existence at the time.

The king had thought his father had discovered his indiscretion with the servant girl, and later that his betrothed's family had something to do with her disappearance. When he exhausted his resources and shifted into a phoenix a year later, he'd married Krish's mother and given up all dreams of a life with Aida.

And now his father was asking the same of him—no, the king was *commanding* it.

It meant everything to Reggie to find his family after twenty-three years of not knowing who he was. But in this moment, he wanted to wish it all away.

I have a betrothed.

Well, more specifically, the future king of Ardu Almaar

had a betrothed. And up until a couple months ago, that had been Krish.

As if he needed another reason for his half-brother to hate him. From what he'd heard from his half-siblings, Krish had been in love with Saraya since they were children, and they'd always planned to marry and unite their kingdoms. Saraya was raised in the Ardu Almaar palace with Krish, having been sent to them by her family when she was only six years old.

To save Saraya's country from financial ruin and potential invasion, a deal was struck for the firstborn prince to wed the firstborn Princess of Pundarika. Ardu Almaar had poured in resources and troops for twelve years to help the tiny island kingdom keep their enemies out.

Reggie felt like the worst kind of usurper.

This was more than problematic. No wonder Krish had tried to kill him. Sort of. But they'd put that sordid ordeal behind them, and Reggie had hoped forgiving his brother unconditionally would change their relationship for the better.

It hadn't.

And now, Reggie knew why.

In the front row, Reggie's girlfriend, Nettie, beamed a smile up at him that could put the sun to shame. Over the last couple months, their relationship had grown serious, and the last thing he wanted to do was tell her they couldn't be together. This would shatter her.

As it was shattering him.

How and when was he supposed to drop something like that on her?

Once Upon Academy
One week later

THIS IS what being a princess at a ball *should* feel like.

Nettie didn't care for balls, having attended more of them in her eighteen years than she could remember. Not a show to put on, or an act to play, and physically and mentally exhausting.

Not the kind of show in the way she performed as a prima ballerina, although ballets could be tedious and full of pressure as well.

Nothing like this one.

At Once Upon Academy's annual Winter Ball, Princess Antoinette Chaikova of Parajsë was just *Nettie*. Surrounded by royals, descendants of fairytale characters, and the magically-talented, Nettie and the others had only to enjoy themselves at this event. There were no dignitaries to impress, no foreign rulers to placate, and no toads to dance with for the sake of "state relations."

No, the only person she'd danced with, wanted to

dance with, and would dance with, was holding her right now.

Reggie's arm was firm around her waist, hugging her and her enormous cloud of a dress as closely as was physically possible. She'd gone for big and poofy out of habit, finding hoops and crinolines to be the perfect natural shield for grabby, narcissistic entitled princes and nobles. But now, when she actually *wanted* to be touched, the billowy layers of white silk and tulle didn't work in her favor.

Next time, no full skirts.

And no elbow-length gloves, either. She'd shucked those off her arms faster than her preschoolers peeled off their ballet slippers at the end of class.

But she was lucky to have a dress at all. She'd missed her appointment with her mother's dressmaker and had to beg the proprietors of Once Upon a Dress Shop in Feydale to make her something really quick. The tailors whipped up the stunning white gown, fit for a winter bride, complete with swan feathers in the trimming and enhanced with a light dusting of rose powder. With Nettie's peaches-and-cream complexion and her long blonde hair up, her roommate and best friend Clara had jokingly called her a snow queen.

Nettie had big expectations for tonight. She would dance and dance and just lose herself in the ambiance of the stunningly decorated ballroom. After Reggie's investiture ceremony, he'd seemed distracted, and Nettie hoped the ball would pull him out of whatever funk he was going through. She sympathized with him; ruling people was a great responsibility, and he'd had zero training.

But he could learn.

And she could help.

The Rockin' Sirens, a talented sister trio, riffed into another slow song, and to Nettie's delight, it was the tune violinist Lyra Piper had been practicing the last few days. Nettie didn't know her dorm neighbor that well—Lyra was a tough nut to crack, and Nettie liked to keep to herself. Until that one night last month when Nettie ventured down to the dorm's theater and found Lyra crying through a sappy Christmas love story. They'd chatted during the commercials and Nettie promised never to breathe a word to anyone about Lyra's secret vice. Several movies later, they'd worked up to a comfortable companionship.

"Aren't the Rockin' Sirens awesome?" Nettie murmured. "Lyra lives next door to Clara and me, and this song has been soothing me all week."

"Mmm." His chin pressed against her temple, the vibrations of his agreement sending a trail of goosebumps from her ear down to her toes.

She closed her eyes and swayed to the melody. Lyra had the voice of an angel. The beautiful lyrics and flowing notes of the song caressed them like a gentle breeze and resonated with her feelings for Reggie.

And in a moment
As the darkness takes hold I can feel in my soul
That there's one thing that will get me through
Get me through
And that's you

Reggie suddenly tensed, gripping Nettie's waist and hand more firmly, expertly steering her closer to the stage. She raised her head to see what could've caused his discomfort and sudden change in direction.

Nearby, his half-brother Krish danced with his girlfriend, Saraya. Though her haunted eyes were unsettling, Nettie didn't think she'd given Saraya any reason not to like her.

Maybe Reggie was tense because he and Krish were still at odds. She could understand that. Krish had been raised to rule, only to find out now he wasn't qualified. He hadn't inherited the ancient gift to shift into a phoenix, and the laws of the kingdom clearly stated the ruler must shift to a phoenix to protect the kingdom. Long ago, Ardu Almaar had been cursed, and without a phoenix, it would not survive. According to the curse, the walls would crumble, the water sources would dry up, and the crops would die. As of yet, no one had tested or challenged that theory.

"You can't avoid him forever, you know," Nettie said gently.

"I can tonight." Reggie tilted his head toward hers until their foreheads were touching.

Nettie lifted her chin and pressed her lips to his. He let go of her hand and tugged her closer, wrapping both his arms around her waist. Her arms encircled his neck, and what started as a gentle kiss quickly became something more.

"You'd better enjoy that now, while you can." Krish's snarky baritone brought Nettie out from under the spell she was under.

"Ignore him," Reggie said, his lips moving along her jaw toward her ear. "You wanna get out of here?"

"Mmm. After this song, though."

Saraya's gentle, rolling accent cut into Lyra's violin solo. "Krish, I am not marrying that man."

What? Nettie raised her head. *Who wasn't marrying who?*

Saraya cradled Krish's face in her hands. Water pooled in her eyes as she spoke gently. "You've always been my king. That hasn't changed, even now, even if it probably should. Clearly, he's in love with someone else, and I'm in love with you."

Wait, what?

Reggie whirled Nettie in a circle, away from the conversing couple. She shook her head and slid her hands down his arms until she was gripping his elbows.

"Reggie, what are they talking about?"

He stiffened again, his expression seizing up, and he didn't answer.

The side of Krish's mouth turned up as he navigated

himself and Saraya so that the couples were beside one another. "You haven't told her, brother?"

A cold chill bubbled up Nettie's spine. "Told me *what,* Reggie?" Nettie squeezed his hand and tried to meet his gaze. Why wouldn't he look at her? Whatever it was, she didn't want to hear it from Krish.

Saraya's eyes widened and she clapped a hand over her mouth.

Krish snorted. Reggie tried to pull Nettie away, but she resisted, keeping a steady gaze on Saraya.

The princess wrung her hands. "I'm so sorry, truly. I thought you knew." She darted a glance at Krish. He gave a slight shake of his head. "I—I thought she knew, Krish! When you said Reggie was choosing the selfish path, I didn't think—"

Nettie tightened her grip on Reggie's arm. *"Tell me."*

Reggie's cool expression twisted into anguish. "I can't say it out loud. That would make it feel too real. Besides, it's *not* going to happen."

Saraya's apologetic expression hardened into anger. "For goodness sake, you can't be a king if you stick your head in the sand when there's a problem you don't know how to fix," she spat. "I'll tell you, Princess Antoinette of Parajsë. The Crown Prince of Ardu Almaar is betrothed to the firstborn princess of Pundarika. And that's *me."*

Nettie sucked in a long breath through her teeth to try to calm the brewing inner turmoil. This couldn't be happening.

"That's right," Krish said, his voice laced with envy and resignation. "And there's nothing he can do about it, because he's the *phoenix*. He can't change or deny the ancient gift, nor can he change or deny the law, and he can't just 'quit.' It's pre-ordained, and it's the *only* way our kingdom can survive. It's time you both accept it."

R eggie pulled at his bowtie and collar, but the action didn't do anything to offset the heat—or the feeling he was being choked. This was *not* how he wanted Nettie to find out about his *duty*. He forced air into his lungs. The cold sweat preceded the burning transformation he was still learning to control.

He needed to get out of this ballroom. *Fast.*

"Reggie? Surely, there's *something* you can do?" Nettie's eyes searched his, looking for confirmation that this was just an archaic tradition—or perhaps a bad dream. "Are you okay?

It'd been his nightmare for the past week.

"That's what *I've* been saying," Saraya poked Krish in his chest. "What *are* you going to do about it? You're both smart. Fix it."

"I have to go. *Now.*" Reggie pulled Nettie toward him

and pressed a frantic kiss to her lips. "It's happening. I can't control it. The heat...I'll find you later. I'm so sorry. About everything" He took a few steps backward and whirled around, leaving her open-mouthed and alone on the dance floor, the unanswered questions on her perfect, rosy-pink lips.

He raced toward the nearest door leading to the patio. He had to get out of the building and far enough away from the guests so he didn't expose himself. Once outside, he sprinted around the couples sprinkled in his way and darted toward the gardens.

Dashing into the passage of tall hedges, he pulled off his tux and under clothes in record time. The skin on his back rippled as the transformation began. The pressure in his upper back and shoulder blades contracted, the shocks lighting up every nerve in his body. Fire consumed his body, and in a moment, the transformation was complete. He lifted into the air, leaving behind a trail of sparks.

Everything was better when he was in flight, soaring above the earth. Distance between himself and the ground made all his problems down there seem small.

Except for this. He couldn't outrun this problem, or view it through another lens. He wasn't just a phoenix; he was *the* phoenix of Ardu Almaar. The only one that mattered to his people. He couldn't be replaced.

Reggie pumped his wings to lift higher, fly faster. His bird's eyes located the astronomy tower, and he glided toward it, slowing to land on the sill of the open stone window.

He hopped down when he was sure the room was empty, and gulped air in long, deep breaths until his heart rate slowed. Closing his eyes, he concentrated on returning to human form. As his body buzzed and tingled, he could only think of Nettie.

Shuffling over to the wall by the door, he located the stone Fairy Godmother had enchanted.

Pressing his palm to it, he recited, "Stone of gray, unlike the rest, reveal the contents of the phoenix's nest."

A fiery red line appeared in the shape of a cross, its glow outlining five bricks. The rocks glimmered, and he dropped his hand as the light brightened then faded away to reveal an enchanted compartment containing his duffle of spare clothes and a sleeping bag.

Reggie reached inside and pulled out the bundle. Relieved of its charge, the bricks moved once more, settling in their original positions as the light extinguished.

The tower wasn't a real nest, per se, but Ms. Fay had been certain he'd need a private place to go when overwhelm took hold of his heart. Activating the spell also put a protection on the tower, allowing only Ms. Fay, the Headmistress, and Nettie access when he was there.

Nettie. He had to find a way to make things right. But first, he needed to sleep and get his strength back. As far as his phoenix lifespan went, he was still a baby, and his body often gave out on him after a strenuous flight.

As Reggie collapsed onto his sleeping bag, he forced himself to think only happy thoughts, drifting off to the memory of holding Nettie close on the dance floor.

IT WAS TOO MUCH.

Once Reggie disappeared out the door, Nettie straightened her shoulders, held her wobbly chin high, and strode toward the powder room. A princess had to keep her composure at all times.

And when she couldn't, that's when she left.

There was no way she'd make it back to her dorm before she either burst into tears or threw up. Clutching her stomach with one hand, she pushed open the door to the ladies' lounge with the other.

She froze at the sight before her. This powder room was already occupied by a crying princess.

Nettie assumed she was a princess. Her dress was so finely made, the fabric alone could have fed a small kingdom for a year.

Perched perfectly on the purple-braid trimmed ivory settee, it appeared a fellow royal was also having herself a night to remember. She looked up, and her water-streaked face caught a glint of light from one of the settee's gold buttons.

We princesses have to look out for each other. Nettie approached her slowly, placing a hand on the curled arm of the settee. "Are you alright? Can I help?"

The stranger continued to cry. Nettie gathered her skirts and sat down beside the weeping young woman. She reached for the other princess's hand, scooped up her fingers, and gave what she thought was a gentle squeeze, but the princess cried out in pain, yanking her hand away.

Nettie's eyes widened. Had she been too forward? "I'm so sorry. Did I hurt you? What can I do?" The princess cried even harder, then took a deep breath. When she'd calmed down, she spoke in a refined tone, but with a noticeable crack. "I'm sorry, it's just that the sensitivity with my hands is what started all this in the first place." She looked up at Nettie. "Why does *everything* have to hurt?"

"Should I call for help? Or should I leave?" Nettie asked.

"No, no—well, I mean, yes, you did hurt me, but it's impossible *not* to hurt me. And it's impossible for me not to hurt others."

Nettie wasn't following, but she thought she should keep the girl talking. It was better than both of them having a cryfest.

Maybe. Sometimes even a princess needed a cryfest. "What happened?"

The princess opened her mouth to speak, but before she could get a sound out, the door burst open and a blur of sparkling black stomped in.

Lyra Piper, sans violin, slammed the door behind her, causing the Pain-Full princess to wince at the sound and vibration.

"Hey..." Lyra stammered, her gaze darting from one girl to the other. "Everybody all right?"

While Nettie thought about how to answer that, Lyra marched to the other side of the

settee.

"Wait, don't touch—" Nettie warned as the other girl gasped.

"I'm sorry!" Lyra squeaked to the yelping princess in a blur of black sparkles as she tried to jump back up mid-sit. Regaining her balance, she kicked off her heels and arranged herself atop the arm of the settee. Leaning further away, she shoved her dress between her legs in an unladylike fashion that would surely set afire the tongues of the dowagers of Parajsë.

Nettie remembered Lyra telling her the dress and heels had been her sisters' idea, and from the way she was acting, it was obvious she was most comfortable wearing more informal attire. Nettie resettled herself on the opposite arm of the settee, just to play it safe.

The distraught royal finally spoke. "You're both upset, too, aren't you? I apologize.

I've been selfish, crying about my problems like this

when it's clear you're both as troubled as I am. And I'm rude as well for not introducing myself. My name is Adeline Augustin-Mignon Sauveterre, Princess of Viasens."

Nettie smiled kindly. "Pleasure to meet you. I'm Antoinette Chaikova, Princess of Parajsë, but you can call me Nettie."

Lyra's eyes darted between the two other girls. "Ooooo-kay. Well, I'm Lyra, of the Piper family, of Boston, Massachusetts, USA." She laughed. "Is that how you introduce yourself all the time? It must be exhausting."

They nodded, and Lyra smiled. "Well, we're all clearly here for the same reason, if our tears are any indication." She turned to Nettie. "You first. What happened out there? Your man took off like something spooked him."

Nettie grimaced. "You saw that?" *Great, if Lyra noticed Reggie leave, so did probably half the school.* She sighed out a long breath and shrugged. "Oh, nothing major. I just learned he's betrothed to another princess."

Adeline gasped. "That sounds awful."

"Holy crap, he's what?" Lyra's eyes slitted. "That's still a thing?"

Nettie shrugged. "Apparently! My kingdom outlawed that barbaric tradition years ago."

Lyra tilted her head to the side. "What's Reggie gonna do about it?"

"I don't think there's anything he *can* do."

Lyra snorted. "Then *you* need to do something about it.

If he's willing to fight for you, that is. That's something special you need to hold onto." She glanced away, and when she continued speaking her voice lost its edge. "That's what I thought I had. This whole time, I thought I meant something to Cole, but he's just been trying to find a way to break up with me." She swung her head back to the others and crossed her arms over her chest. "Enough about me and my stupid reaper boyfriend." She leaned toward Adeline, careful not to touch her. "What's your story?"

Adeline hung her head. "I thought what I had with Quilo was special, but we can't be together. Not because of any laws, but because we're too different."

"I don't understand," Nettie said.

"Well, I'm sure by now you've discovered my sensitivities. My—I mean, Quilo has powers over ice and snow. How can we possibly have a relationship that will thrive when we can't even touch each other's hands without hurting each other? His cold hands hurt me, and hurting me hurts *him*."

Lyra let out a low whistle. "That wicked sucks."

Adeline's lips twitched as she wiped at her tears. "It does, it does."

Nettie couldn't hold her own tears in any longer. It did seem as if they were fated to be in this room together. Three poor pretty princesses—well, Lyra wasn't technically a princess, but she played the violin like one who'd been royally trained—dumped by their prince charmings.

"Oh, no!" Adeline cried. "I didn't mean to make you cry all over again!"

Lyra glared at them and shook her head. "This is a freakin' magical academy. Your guys want to be with you, and you two want to be with them, right? Figure it out, people, figure it out!"

A squeak of metal cut her off, and the three of them darted their gazes to the door. An elaborately-dressed royal in a sparkling midnight blue dress, her hair upswept in thick curls, slunk in. She held a pair of emerald green gloves in her hand.

"There you are, Adeline! I've been looking everywhere for you. It's way past midnight. You need your gloves." She handed the gloves to Adeline. "I just saw Quilo leave. What's going on?"

"I—I think we've just broken up, Mirella."

"Oh, honey, I'm so sorry. Let me take you home. You need some warm cocoa and fluffy blankets and to get out of those shoes."

"I think that's wise." Adeline stood, nodding to Lyra and Nettie. "Thank you both for everything. I hope the next time we meet will be under more pleasant circumstances." She gave them a dainty wave.

Mirella held the door open and mouthed *thank you* at Lyra and Nettie on her way out.

A buzzing sounded from Lyra's dress. She fussed with the folds, muttering under her breath, and pulled out a cell phone. "I guess I have to go out and face the music. Are you going to be okay? Can we talk later?"

Nettie nodded. "Yeah. I just need some time alone."

"I'll see you back at the dorm. We'll make a date with Ben and Jerry."

"Ugh, more boys?"

Lyra flashed a grin as she opened the door. "Trust me, you'll love them."

Nettie didn't know about that. She did need to find Clara, though.

And get the heck out of this ballroom.

CHAPTER

THREE

Ardu Almaar Palace
Late December

"I don't want this, Krish." Reggie rubbed his eyes and blinked over the ancient tome as if it held the answers they were searching for. "We both stand to lose what matters most to us if I become king."

Krish folded his arms and leaned on a nearby book-shelf in the palace's library. "You don't get it, brother. What matters *most* is the kingdom. Not our hearts, or who holds them. Duty, above all else." He spat the last words out with a sneer. "The king is the phoenix. The phoenix is the king. It's been that way for centuries."

"But what if I hadn't been found? What then?" Reggie scrubbed at his several-days-old beard. He hadn't shaved or bathed since he left Once Upon Academy for Winter

Break. After he left the ball, he'd flown to the astronomy tower, where he'd fallen asleep, exhausted. Nettie had found him there the next morning, and had been more understanding than he would have expected—or deserved. She loved him; he had no doubt about that. And she believed with her whole heart that their love was enough of a reason to change the law.

Only, the law wasn't his to change.

Nor was it his father's. When he'd approached his father about it, the king had confessed his health was failing, and if he could amend the curse, he would have. He hadn't been able to shift since Reggie's first transformation. The king's mortality clock was ticking, and his family had no idea. When they found out, they would blame Reggie for that, too. His heart ached for his half-siblings, who stood to lose their dad, and for himself, who'd just found his father.

Despite Reggie's insistence to forgo graduate studies in Kingdom Management at OUA, his father had insisted Reggie return to school the following semester to learn the basics of what he'd need to know to govern their people.

Reggie would comply, but he'd also spend every spare minute trying to find a way to shift the phoenix powers to his brother, and pray that by doing so, he'd also buy his father more time.

Krish stood and shrugged. "I've learned the laws of this kingdom inside and out. If there's a way to change anything, it would need to be through magic. Either by reversing the curse or finding a way to counter it, there may be a small chance to change our fates. But there's no record of when the curse began or from whom it came. Clever of the curser to leave us without a starting point, eh?"

Reggie grimaced. "I'll just have to be cleverer."

Krish's hollow laugh echoed throughout the chamber as he left the room. Reggie closed the Book of Laws and returned it to its place on the podium in the center of the library.

Magic. Perhaps he was looking in the wrong library.

Once Upon Academy
Early January

NETTIE ARRIVED BACK on campus a few days before the spring term started. After a quick stop to her room, she left the dorm for the library. Reggie had some news, and he'd asked her to meet him there.

He'd told her not to get her hopes up that they'd find a solution, but she was confident there had to be a way around the curse. This was Once Upon Academy, after all, a place full of students and alumni who were famous for breaking curses. Why would Reggie's situation be any different?

She rounded the corner and smiled as she noticed him waiting for her by the entrance. Since they met last semester, his shoulders had widened and his wiry athletic frame had bulked up to bodyguard-like proportions. She'd never felt safer or more protected than when she was in those strong arms, with their hearts beating in tandem in a song that was only theirs.

Failing to find a solution was not an option. They were each other's forever, and no curse was going to get in the way of that.

They would either break it or die trying.

Reggie caught her gaze and the butterflies within her kicked into high gear. She grinned and picked up her pace as he held out his arms. She crashed into him and hugged him close.

"That was the longest two weeks ever!" She rubbed her face in his chest. "Let's never be apart that long again."

He rubbed her shoulder and kissed the top of her head. "Deal."

Nettie loosened her arms just enough to pull her head back and look up at him. "Seal it with a kiss?"

"Is there any other way?" He grinned; his lips silencing her giggle as their lips met. She closed her eyes and let her concerns melt away for the duration of the kiss.

"No way is Saraya getting anywhere near those lips of yours," Nettie teased, hoping to make Reggie smile.

"Not as long as I'm breathing," he growled.

Nettie elbowed him. "Don't make jokes like that. Anything can—and does—happen in this realm."

He grinned. "Sorry. You ready?"

"Let's go."

They entered through the ornate door and Reggie led her to the Ancient Magic section. "Krish said the only way around the curse would be magic. This seems like a good place to start."

Book after book, hour after hour, they read and searched for ways to break and counter curses. This curse, that curse; none were even similar to the fate that had been bestowed upon Ardu Almaar.

When the announcement came that the library would close in five minutes, Nettie noticed droplets of sweat beading at Reggie's hairline. "You okay, Reg?"

His face flushed and he shook his head. "I have to go." He stood up quickly and emptied his pockets. "Meet me at the tower?"

Nettie nodded, recognizing the signs that he was about to shift. "Go, go! I'll put these books away."

"Thanks!" She watched him sprint away, hoping he made it outside in time. He glanced back, and her gaze caught his. Heat filled her cheeks.

"Go!"

Once he was out the door, Nettie tossed Reggie's things into her tote and rolled up his jacket, placing it on top. She returned the books to the shelves. When she put the last one away, a title caught her eye. *Gold and its Effects on Incantations: A Thesis.* The thin, frail book appeared to glimmer in the fluorescent lighting.

Gold? She read the back cover and quickly skimmed through the book. Almost one hundred years old, it had been written and researched by former student, Ritvik of Pundarika, who'd successfully broken several curses with a wand he'd turned to gold with a philosopher's stone.

Pundarika! Saraya's kingdom?

"Attention students. The library is now closed. Please exit the building. Thank you."

She was out of time. Nettie pulled on her coat and scanned the aisle for anyone who might be watching. Discreetly, she shoved the book into her tote bag, slung it over her shoulder, and raced out of the building.

FOUR

The rigid, cool stonework of the inner tower wall against Reggie's bare human back was a welcome relief from the flaming heat within that came with his transformations.

He had to get this under control. His father had told him he'd master the shifts once he'd mastered his emotions. He'd been working for months and had even made it through the investiture without incident, so why had he been unable to control tonight's change and the one at the ball?

Reggie pulled himself to his feet and sought out the enchanted bricks. Pressing his hand onto the center stone of the magical large rectangles, he closed his eyes and recited the incantation.

The slamming of the heavy door at the base of the tower signaled Nettie's arrival. Reggie retrieved his stuff from the recess and quickly pulled on his jeans and hoodie. Still barefoot, he opened the door to the observatory level just as Nettie reached the landing, breathing heavy as if she'd ran the entire way.

She met his eyes and smiled with excitement. "I think I may have found something."

A blip of hope danced in his chest as she lifted to press a kiss to his lips. She tugged him over to the open window and they sat in the spotlight of the moon's glow. "What did you find?"

Nettie pulled a large, thin book from her bag. "Look at this!"

His eyes scanned the title. "I don't understand."

"Look at the author." Her command carried excitement, not the seriousness he expected.

He lowered his eyes back to the cover and sucked in a breath. "Ritvik of *Pundarika.*"

"Saraya's kingdom. We need to find this guy, see what he knows. Maybe he can lend us the wand!"

Reggie's shoulders dropped. "If he's alive."

She leaned forward, her eyes sparkling. "At your investiture, there was a very old man seated with Saraya's parents. I swear someone addressed him as Lord Ritvik! If it wasn't him, they must be related, no?"

"I do remember him. Saraya's great uncle."

A tingle inched its way up Reggie's spine. Nettie handed him his phone. "Call Krish."

NETTIE TWISTED her fingers together under the heavy cloak and snuck a side glance at Reggie, seated beside her in one of OUA's magical carriages. He'd held her hand until she couldn't stand the heat and pulled it out of his clammy grip.

She'd seen him like this many times now. His rigid posture and stoic expression belied the battle he was fighting within. Shifting now, as they approached a side entrance at his family's palace, would be the worst possible timing.

The horses slowed to a stop and the door swung open. Instead of the OUA footman, it was Krish on the other side. He raised a finger to his lips and then reached up to take Nettie's hand to assist her down the steps.

When Reggie's feet touched the ground, the soft whoosh of a breeze lifted Nettie's hair.

She looked back as the carriage disappeared into the night as if it'd never been there.

They followed Krish inside and down a long hall which Nettie recognized as the guest wing she'd stayed in when she and her parents attended the Investiture events. Krish stopped at the last door on the left, knocked twice, and then once more after a pause.

The door opened inward, and Saraya poked her head out. Her smooth jet-black hair fell in waves down to her waist, a dark contrast falling over her traditional orange sari. A beautiful multifaceted ruby in the center of her forehead caught the hall light.

"Come in, but quietly. He's watching *Jeopardy!* in the next room and doesn't like interruptions. We can wait here in the parlor."

"Who's in jeopardy?" Nettie asked, her heartbeat picking up its pace. "Are we—?" She cast her wide eyes at Krish.

He smirked. "It's an American game show."

"Game show?" She wasn't following.

"On the television."

"Ah!" Nettie nodded and made a mental note to ask Lyra about it the next time she saw her. She tightened her grip on her tote bag and sunk onto the nearest settee. She wasn't sure if she should remove her cloak. "How much longer?"

Saraya pointed to the clock. "Ten minutes."

Reggie joined Nettie on the settee and leaned forward, resting his forearms on his thighs. Heat was still emanating from him, and Nettie wished she knew how to help him better manage his gift.

Or curse, depending on who one talked to. Reggie would give anything to be rid of the trait, but Nettie wasn't so sure. She herself had the power to shift into a swan, a trait that had also been born of a curse, but she'd come to appreciate the majesty of it.

"Can I see the book?" Krish asked. Nettie pulled it from her tote and handed to him. "Sary?"

Saraya was at his side in a second, her eyes raking over the cover. She snatched it from him and opened the book. "Ugh! This was written by Uncle Ritvik's *father*. He's been gone a long time. Disappeared in Albania decades ago. Dammit!"

"Your uncle still may know something." Krish's voice held a note of desperation. "The wand is our only lead right now."

Saraya handed it back to him. "I'm sorry." She brushed a lock of hair off his forehead and pressed a light kiss to his lips. "I just don't see a way out of this, and every time I get my hopes up, it's a dead end."

"Every time?" Reggie asked, impatience laced in his question. "When else? You've tried other things? What are you keeping from us?"

"If there was something to share, I would have told you, brother." Krish practically spat the words. "I hired a detective of sorts to help us." He held up his hand as Reggie's mouth opened. "He'll be discreet, I can assure you."

"'Detective of sorts?'" Nettie asked suspiciously. "You didn't hire a Brennington, did you?"

Krish averted her sharp gaze. "What else was there to do? They're the most successful anthropological researchers in all the realms."

Nettie couldn't believe it. "And the most expensive. What did they want from you? Your firstborn?"

"It doesn't matter."

"What is she talking about, Krish?" Reggie asked. "What price did you pay?"

Saraya's frown indicated she hadn't been part of the deal-making. "He only pays if they figure it out. Which is why *we* must do it first." A clock chimed half past the hour. "Follow me."

In the adjoining room, the old wrinkled man switched off the television and closed his eyes. Saraya rushed over to him and laid a hand on the sleeve of his silk bathrobe. "Uncle Ritvik, please, we only need a few minutes of your time."

He opened his eyes, his gaze sweeping over the two couples, and sucked in a long loud breath. "The phoenix and the swan!" He gasped, his eyes, bugging out. "The dark prince and the lotus blossom!" Nettie stared open-mouthed and relaxed into the recliner. "So, the prophecy has been fulfilled."

His eyes snapped shut.

R eggie counted in his head, focusing on long, even breathing. *In, two, three, four. Out, two three, four. Stay human, stay human.* He balled his fists and squeezed.

"What prophecy?" Krish demanded, his eyes flashing the irritation Reggie felt.

"Uncle Ritvik!" Saraya shook the old man. "He's not breathing!"

Krish was on the old man's other side in a blink, pressing his fingers to the side of his neck. "No pulse," he reported through clenched teeth. "Reggie, help me get him on the floor."

Reggie snapped to attention, and together, the two of them lifted the elderly man out of the chair and onto the floor. He watched in horror as Krish performed CPR multiple times with no improvement.

Behind them, Saraya spoke into a speaker on the wall, alerting the palace medical team and providing details. Krish sat back on his heels and dropped his face in his hands.

Reggie scanned for Nettie, finding her straddling the open doorway. Her lips were pressed tightly together, the only sign that she was ruffled. Calm, composed, and steady was her way, in every situation. She'd become his rock.

Their eyes locked, and the fiery heat within him that usually indicated a shift cooled to a comfortable warmth. Instinctively, he turned back to Saraya's uncle and placed his hand over the man's heart. His fingers began to tingle, but he kept them steady. A faint beating registered beneath his hand, becoming steadier with each passing second.

"Krish." Reggie whispered so as to not alert the girls. "Breathe into him."

His brother's hands fell, revealing red-rimmed, blood-shot eyes. "What's the point?"

Reggie's heart clenched at the despair in Krish's question. "His heart's beating."

"What?" Krish returned his fingers to the man's neck. His eyes widened. "How?" He didn't wait for an answer. Gently opening Lord Ritvik's mouth, he leaned down and gave him the breath of life.

Reggie's hand felt like it was burning from the inside. The old man coughed into Krish's mouth, his eyes opening briefly, then closing again. Krish flew backward, his expression dazed.

The old man spoke in a thin voice. "It has been foretold. You all must...work together...The bird of paradise... phoenix...find the blue bird to change the..."

"Change the what?" Reggie asked.

There was a commotion at the door as Security and two members of the palace's medical team burst through with a stretcher and equipment. Reggie stepped back and didn't look away until the oxygen mask was placed over Lord Ritvik's face, hoping until the last second he'd say more. What had he been getting at?

Phoenix, swan, and now a bird of paradise and a bluebird? Images swirled through Reggie's mind, an aviary of birds taunting him. Getting close, only to turn and fly away. He shook his head to clear it.

Nettie positioned herself beside him and took his hand in hers, squeezing it gently. He squeezed back as they watched the team work to get the old man's vitals stable.

The paramedic closest to Reggie and Nettie shouted into his shoulder radio. "Prepare the king's helicopter for medevac. We need to go now!" He nodded to his partner, and they lifted the stretcher to waist-height.

"What's happening to Uncle Ritvik?" Saraya cried, pushing past Krish to get to the stretcher.

The second responder turned toward her, effectively blocking Saraya's access. "Your Highness, please, clear the path!" she commanded.

"But—"

"You can meet us at the hospital," the first paramedic's expression softened. "Legally, I can't tell you anything. We've been instructed to report only to the king."

They wheeled the stretcher out and they heard the outside door to the suite bang shut. An awkward silence filled the room.

"Let's go, Sary," Krish prompted softly. "I'll sort this out with Father."

"Krish, he has to be okay." Tears pooled in her eyes. "I—we—we have to find a way to be together." Her face crumpled. "It sounded like he knew something that could help us."

Nettie, having been quiet for the entirety of the ordeal, now spoke with conviction. "I'm sure you're right, Saraya. Let's go now so we'll be there if he becomes able to speak again."

Reggie slipped his fingers from hers and snaked an arm around her waist, pulling her close. She turned her face to his and the true urgency of the situation passed between them. They both seemed to know the old man didn't have much time left.

Nettie paced the hospital's waiting room. Surely, a kingdom with a palace the size of Ardu Almaar's should have a hospital wing. It was basic security protocol for the royal family to have emergency and surgical capabilities on site. So why the airlift to the Capitol's facility?

What made the paramedics decide to airlift the dignitary from Pundarika to a separate location for treatment? Did Lord Ritvik have a pre-existing condition that couldn't be treated in the privacy of the palace, or were the attending doctors unable to get to him quickly enough? Why was the king the only person who was allowed to know of his condition? Surely, Saraya, being family, deserved courtesy update, at least.

"You're going to wear a track in the floor," Krish said to her.

Saraya whirled at the midpoint of her path and stalked over to him. "You! Surely, you, who has been trained since birth to rule this kingdom, should find this situation unusual. I wasn't groomed to be a king, but even *I* know when something seems off."

Krish raised his chin to meet her gaze, holding it steady as he spoke softly. "What do you expect me to do about it?"

Reggie held up his hands. "Enough arguing! This isn't helping. Let's prepare for the worst, just in case. If Lord Ritvik dies, he at least left us a clue. We can start on that while we wait for an update. If he recovers, awesome. If not, well, then at least we didn't waste time."

"Spoken like a leader," Saraya observed. She pressed

her lips together and nodded. "I'd like to go home. I think I know where to start."

"Sary, we've already scoured the palace library. There's nothing there," Krish said.

"Not the palace," she said. "My birthplace. Pundarika."

"No. I'll go," Krish said.

"But—you have school, Krish. Really, I'll be safe. The Ardu Almaar Guard haven't let anything happen to my family since they took over security ten years ago."

Krish was adamant. "It's too much of a risk. I'd die if anything happened to you."

Nettie, touched by Krish's declaration to Saraya, turned to Reggie. "We should all go."

"It's too dangerous." Krish insisted. "Reggie and I can handle it."

Before Nettie or Saraya could object, the door to the waiting room opened, and Nettie recognized Hani, one of the king's personal guards. His usual frown was even more pronounced, giving him and even grimmer countenance than usual.

"The king has asked me to report that the medical staff was unable to maintain Lord Ritvik's vital signs. They have placed him on life support until The King of Pundarika arrives so that he may make the final decision." He spun on his heel and left them in stunned silence.

Saraya twisted in her chair and buried her face in Krish's shirt. Nettie fought the urge to comfort her as she sobbed silently.

Keep a cool head. Chin up. Use your authority to command every situation. Her mother's words echoed in her ears.

Nettie set her shoulders back. "It's evident time is of utmost importance. Krish, you and Saraya go to Pundarika. Her uncle's death and his return to his homeland may give you an opportunity to search his personal effects. Reggie and I will request a meeting with Ms. Fay and perhaps she can provide some guidance. I'm confident that working together will lead us to a solution at the soonest possible time."

They all nodded their agreement and Reggie pulled her aside. "That was incredible, the way you just took charge there. You're going to make a fine queen someday, Nettie," he said sadly.

Nettie fought a smile and reached up to cup his cheek in her hand, caressing his soft trimmed shadowbeard. He leaned into her palm and closed his eyes. It didn't seem right to express happiness when a man had just died. "If I must rule something, it'll be by your side. But let's not count our eggs before they've hatched."

Outside the Once Upon Academy library, Reggie checked his phone for the tenth time. Odd. Nettie was never late.

Maybe he should call her.

But if she was late, it was because she had a good reason. Or she would just call or text to let him know.

Right?

He stared at the screen and sighed, willing it to light up with a notification.

"That's a serious frown you have on your face. Careful, or it might freeze that way." Reggie jumped at Lyra Piper's invasion of his thoughts.

"Waiting for your girl?" she asked.

He gave a slight nod and cleared his throat. "Hey, Lyra."

"Hey, yourself." She narrowed her eyes and pursed her

lips. "Doesn't she have alchemy today? If it was last period, she's probably still there helping clean up after the explosion."

Reggie stiffened as a sharp shock zapped him internally. "Explosion! Is she okay? Were you there?"

Lyra shrugged. "Nope, heard about it walking over here. No serious injuries is the rumor." She quirked a brow. "Here's a thought. Maybe you should *call* her."

"Uhh…" He averted her pointed stare. "I'll just head over there. I could help."

Lyra rolled her eyes. "Men." Before he could answer, she breezed by him. He winced as the heavy door slammed in her wake.

Reggie shoved his phone in his pocket and took off in a jog toward the science labs. As he neared the entrance to the building, the door swung open and a group of students burst out. He scanned their faces. No Nettie, but he caught sight of her roommate.

"Clara!" He raised his hand in a wave.

The petite blonde waved back and yelled, "She's still in class!" before turning toward the dorms.

"Thanks!"

Reggie bounded up the steps and caught the door from the last of the students exiting. It had been years since he'd taken alchemy, so he hoped the classroom location hadn't changed.

A minute later, he arrived at the closed door to the alchemy lab. Professor Auden Peabody's loud squeaky voice projected through the door. He didn't sound angry, though. More...excited?

The perimeter around the door glowed with a sparking aura, indicating it was magically locked. Reggie knocked three times and held his breath.

The glittering seal darkened, and then disappeared. The door opened, revealing the stout old professor, who was rumored to be over two hundred years old. He stood on top of his desk amid piles of books and papers.

"Ah! Just the chap we've been discussing. Come in, come in!"

Stunned, Reggie entered the classroom, which was in a state of total disarray. His eyes landed on Nettie among the overturned tables, broken chairs, and shattered glass. Covered in patches of soot and liquid gold, she smiled smugly as she met his quizzical gaze.

Professor Peabody shuffled back to the only erect table, which Nettie was standing behind. "Our Nettie here has an aptitude for alchemy! Only one student of mine has ever successfully turned granite into gold, and that was over a hundred years ago!" The old man's log white beard jumped as he giggled with pride.

"Did you say over a hundred years ago, professor?" Reggie's chest thumped as his brain scrambled to comprehend the implications of this new piece of information.

"Why, yes, I did. He was quite the chemist, quite the chemist!" Reggie exchanged a glance with Nettie.

"Was it Ritvik of Pundarika?" he asked.

"Yes!" The professor leaned toward him, his spectacles sliding down his nose. He stroked his cloud white beard. "Made quite the wand out of it, too. He was determined to be a great wizard."

"What happened to him?" Reggie asked.

"Why, he became a great wizard, of course!" The professor blinked at him, as if it was the most obvious thing.

"I'm not sure how this all connects." Reggie's head swam with uncommented thoughts and details. It all still seemed impossible.

"Nettie here was explaining the reasons behind her happy accident—we were not working with granite today, you see, so she was off task and then the explosion, and well..."

He trailed off. Nettie flashed him a smile, then turned to Reggie. She tucked a lock of hair behind her ear. "I'm sorry I missed our library meeting. I wanted to see if I could make a wand like the one we're looking for. I didn't get it right, but I think I'm on the right track. Right professor?"

He beamed back at her and raised his index finger straight into the air. "If you haven't, we will try until we do!"

Reggie ran a hand through his hair. "But how can the ability to make gold fight a curse?"

"My boy," the professor explained. "Curses are compli-cated. Death is a curse that goes back to the beginning of time. You can prolong life and reverse the curse when the right sort of magic, through a conductor, is used. Take me, for example. I'm two hundred-and-forty-seven years young. The curse was reversed!"

"But is it permanent?" Reggie asked. "Will you never die?"

"Not as long as the counter curse is in effect."

Reggie's mind swam. "So what's next?"

Nettie bit her lip and slid a circlet of stretchy fabric from her wrist, pulling her hair back into a long ponytail. "We update Saraya and Krish. Maybe this can help them with their research in Pundarika, which will bring us closer to a solution. We're still missing the philosopher's stone element that can alter curses."

Reggie picked up Nettie's tote bag and slung it on his shoulder and reached for her hand. "Do you think it's possible, professor, to transfer my birthright magically, where there's a curse involved?"

"My boy," the professor winked. "Anything is possible at Once Upon Academy."

Nettie gave Reggie's hand one more squeeze for good measure as they walked out of the building. Professor Peabody assured them he'd take care of the mess, but she still felt bad for blowing up the lab. "Thanks for carrying my bag."

He stopped when their footsteps touched the ground and gave her arm a gentle yank. "Happy to," he said, pulling her toward him.

She lifted on her toes and pressed her lips to his. Feeling the blush warm her cheeks, she lowered her lashes as she settled back on her heels. "I love you," she whispered, wrapping her arms around his waist and resting her head on his chest. "I really hope we can reverse this before it's too late."

"Me, too." His arms tightened around her. "Where do you want to meet with Krish and Saraya? Pundarika isn't safe..."

Nettie stepped back. "I know you want to protect me, Reggie, but I have to go. Of the four of us, I'm the most knowledgeable about this." She gave a dry laugh. "How crazy is that?"

"Pretty crazy." He hugged her closer. "Okay. But let's wait until after class Friday, and let me set it up and come with you. We'll make a weekend of it. I'll call Krish after I walk you back to your dorm to, ah, change." Nettie snorted, and he laughed. "They can send a guard to escort us to Pundarika."

Her brow furrowed. "Is it really that bad there? I asked my brother about the state of Saraya's country, and he said it's never been safer. For the last ten years, they haven't had any major problems with invaders."

"That we know of." Reggie's lips pressed into a grim line. "From my understanding, it's all thanks to the presence of our soldiers. The threats are still there. They've thwarted assassination attempts on the royal family more than a few times. That's one of the reasons the daughters have been sent away to marry into kingdoms with powerful military resources. Saraya's brothers, as heirs to the throne, rarely leave the palace complex, just as a precaution."

Nettie's eyes widened. "I had no idea. How horrible to grow up so far away from your family or to be a prisoner in your own house." Her heart went out to Saraya and her siblings, and Nettie found herself reflecting. Maybe her mother's meddling wasn't so bad, compared to what her life could have been like.

"Truly, the island kingdom's position puts it in danger, and its ports are envied by friends and enemies alike. It's a big risk to go there, even briefly." Reggie reached for her, circling his arms around her waist. "We have to be careful and vigilant."

"I understand." Nettie tipped up her chin to meet his kiss. The soft pillowy feel of his lips was all the security she needed.

SEVEN

Reggie hadn't known what to expect, but it certainly wasn't anything as grandiose as the massive structure they'd just flown over. He fought his natural urge to shift, and hoped he got a chance someday to explore the kingdom in his avian form.

The Lotus Palace, where the royal family spent their winters, was high in the small mountain range near the north shore. The structure was built into the side of the highest peak, Mount Bengalla, and connected to a series of tunnels inside the rocky terrain. Being the highest point on the island, the peak was off-limits to citizens and international recreational climbers; instead housing the kingdom's main security resources and communication center.

When the OUA carriage touched down, it was immediately surrounded by a heavily-armed guard that had assembled on the front lawn awaiting their arrival. The two soldiers who had accompanied Nettie and Reggie, one each a native of Ardu Almaar and Pundarika, respectively, stood, but motioned for them to stay seated.

"A precaution, your Royal Highnesses." Cheduba, the Pundarikan guard explained. "We must make sure the welcoming unit has not been compromised."

"Is that protocol, or are you expecting a threat?" Nettie asked.

"In the ten years I've served here, there have always been threats, however, this is straight protocol," Telavi, the other soldier, explained.

Reggie tracked him as he positioned himself by the door and spoke in a language he didn't understand. Unable to tell if it was Ardu Almaarin or Pundarikan, it was another reminder of how out of his element he was. Each day, it became more imperative to find a way to break the curse so that Krish could do the job he was raised for—the job Reggie didn't want.

Telavi nodded to Cheduba, who joined him at the door and tapped three times. It was pulled open by the Once Upon Academy footman. A vibrant shade of orange carpet was rolled up the steps, and Cheduba exited first.

After a moment, Telavi motioned to Nettie. She stood and moved to the door. Glancing back at Reggie with a small smile, she extended her gloved hand to the footman to assist her down the steps.

"Your Royal Highness." Telavi bowed his head. Reggie

didn't think he'd ever get used to being addressed as such. "I sense your discomfort. I assure you the palace is secure. Your brother and Her Royal Highness the Princess Saraya are waiting for you just inside the Great Room's doors. I've been assigned to be your personal guard for the duration of your stay, and my wife, Elie, will guard Her Royal Highness, the Princess Antoinette. We are both highly trained and ranked in the Ardu Almaarian Guard."

"I've no doubt you'll do whatever it takes to keep us safe, and I'm grateful. Thank you." Telavi nodded and gestured for Reggie to proceed. He exited the carriage, shaking his head. He was sure he sounded like a fraud, never knowing if he was saying the right thing in the right way.

Nettie waited for him beside a female soldier, whom he assumed was Elie. Her dark hair was pulled back into a knot at her nape and aviator sunglasses hid her eyes. She was dressed in the same tan cargo pants, combat boots, and black armored vest as the men.

Reggie extended his arm to Nettie, and Telavi and Elie flanked their side as they proceeded along the carpet and up the steps of the white marble building. Above, two armed soldiers stood at attention on the balcony that surrounded an enormous golden dome.

Once through the arched main entrance, Reggie quickened his pace as his gaze caught Krish's. He and Saraya were in formal Pundarikan attire, standing stiffly among a dozen attendants.

"Something tells me this won't be the quick visit I envisioned," Reggie muttered into Nettie's ear.

She giggled softly. "No sneaking into this palace, that's for sure."

"Brother. Your Royal Highness." Krish greeted them in an authoritative tone. Reggie was again reminded of Krish's upbringing, and was impressed that at only eighteen years of age, how commanding a presence he was.

Nettie curtsied, and Reggie wondered if he was supposed to bow. Technically, he outranked Krish, but they were in another kingdom. He dipped his head in Saraya's direction as an afterthought.

"Welcome to Pundarika." Saraya greeted them warmly. "I hope your journey here was satisfactory. Your rooms have been readied, and the staff will accompany you there. A formal dinner with their Royal Majesties, the King and Queen, who have just returned from Lord Ritvik's funeral, as well as the Prince Regent will be served at seven." Her gaze darted between them, a glint in her eyes. "After that, we'll change into something more comfortable and entertain ourselves for the rest of the evening."

Nettie nodded and squeezed Reggie's arm gently. He cleared his throat. "Yes, er, that sounds great." Saraya smiled kindly. He felt like a fool. "Thank you."

Nearly two hours until dinner, which would likely last another two hours if they were lucky. Welcoming dinners were known to last well into the night. The trappings of royalty felt like a vice squeezing his independence. So much wasted time. He covered Nettie's hand with his own, grateful for the extra strength her mere touch provided.

DINNER WAS A LAVISH AFFAIR. Nettie had met the King and Queen of Pundarika on several occasions, but had never spoken with them past formal greetings in receiving lines. They welcomed her and Reggie like old friends, and despite their cheerful countenance, she could tell from the lines in their faces and frequent glances to the guards that they were concerned about something they weren't sharing. They wished the quartet well in their efforts to find a way to reverse the curse, and offered to provide any and all assistance needed.

Saraya had confided in Nettie while they were in Ardu Almaar that her parents were worried about Reggie's inexperience, as well as their daughter's new predicament. With their benefactor ailing and his son untrained, they feared their enemies would take advantage if given the opportunity. Krish was young, and Saraya even younger, but even if the king passed prematurely, the citizens of the island kingdom felt more secure with Krish on the throne than the new, inexperienced heir.

As she changed into black leggings, an oversized loose

pink sweater and ballet flats, Nettie thought of their secondary mission, praying that there was a way to break the curse without having to strip Reggie of his shifting ability. Now that he'd embraced that part of himself and was learning to control it, she feared it would make him feel less than he did now without it.

Accompanied by Elie, she waited for the others on a sofa by the elevator bank at the end of the third-floor hall. Above them, in an elaborate light fixture, several cameras disguised as decorative glass cylinders caught every angle of the hall.

Turning her head up to Elie, who stood next to the couch, Nettie placed a hand over her face and pretended to stifle a yawn. "Is there this much security everywhere? I didn't find any cameras in my room."

"Mm," Elie confirmed. She pulled a cylinder of lip balm from one of the pockets in her pants and spoke while she swiped it across her lips. "There are cameras in your room. Voice activated by a code word. I turned them off while you were changing."

Nettie sucked in a loud breath and concentrated on keeping her expression neutral. "May I use your lip balm?"

Elie smiled and passed it to her. "Certainly, your Royal Highness."

Nettie mimicked what Elie had done while she answered, though she kept the stick from actually touching her lips. "Shouldn't I be privy to the code in case you become indisposed?"

"Mm." Elie looked down as she replaced the tube in her pocket. "I'll have to get clearance for that."

"Most appreciated." Nettie leaned back into the couch and wondered what was taking Reggie so long. His room was across from hers.

The elevator dinged, and Krish and Saraya stepped out with their guards. Nettie rose to her feet, watching Krish's eyes focus on the hall ahead. Reggie's door opened, and Krish's shoulders relaxed. Nettie smiled to herself, touched at Krish's relief. It was a big change from only a few months ago, when Krish's actions had almost resulted in Reggie's death.

Saraya spoke as Reggie joined their tight circle. "Thank you for joining us for a tour of the palace. I believe we'll start from the bottom up."

Nettie reached for Reggie's hand. He set his shoulders back and nodded at Krish, understanding they were not free to speak. "Understood. Lead the way."

They took an elevator down several flights, deep into the mountain's base. The doors opened to reveal a brightly lit hallway, its white walls draped in finely woven tapestries picturing vignettes of the daily life of the island's ancient inhabitants. Six soldiers, three on each side of the hall, stood at attention along an ornate oriental rug that stretched the length of the corridor, ending with a set of double doors.

"This hall leads to our archives and most valuable treasures. I do hope you enjoy your tour." Saraya spoke loudly, no doubt for the purpose of being overheard by the security personal and technology.

The four, led by Krish and Saraya's guards with Telavi and Elie behind them, proceeded down the narrow hall. When they reached the door, Saraya's guard entered a code into a pad on the wall and pressed her palm to the screen. A laser scanned her face and metal gears began moving within the doors.

With a final click, the door unlocked. Krish's guard opened it and spoke briefly to a guard on the other side, then motioned for the others to follow him.

The guards led them past row after row of shelves stocked with artifacts to a door beneath a winding staircase directly opposite of where they entered.

Saraya moved to the front of the group to stand by the door. "Your Royal Highnesses, welcome. It's our pleasure entirely to share our most precious artifacts with you. Before your formal tour of the archives and treasure room, I will first explain all the rules for your visit and tell you the history of our great island nation. Please, enter and make yourselves comfortable."

Nettie and Reggie entered hand-in-hand and sat on the nearest sofa. Krish and Saraya sat across a coffee table in matching high-back upholstered chairs. The guards stood silently by each of their charges.

Saraya gathered them into a tight circle just inside the entrance. "We have news to share, so we brought you here where we cannot be overheard. We couldn't speak freely in the hall."

She introduced Nettie and Reggie to the man and woman guarding her and Krish. "Denpo, Pemala, Telavi, and Elie can be trusted. I'll not speak for anyone else, nor recommend even speaking to others."

"I'm sorry it has to be this way," Saraya apologized. She closed her eyes briefly as if to gather strength. "It is very different here than it is in your kingdoms, no? Alas, it must be, at least until we can be assured of the island's perpetual security." She glanced at Krish. He reached over to hold her hand looked at her with a level of care and admiration Nettie hadn't been expecting. She knew Krish cared for Saraya, but seeing him now, in her home, with so much at stake, resolved Nettie to focus even harder on finding a solution.

Krish's expression softened from the stern façade he'd projected up to this point. "Be cool, brother; move and act with authority. Follow my lead if you become unsure. Showing weakness or indecision of any kind will foster doubt, or worse, dissent. The people of Pundarika must see you as a strong ally and capable leader."

"Are you sure the wand's not here?" Nettie asked. Reggie scanned the interior of the cavernous room. Carved shelves displaying ornate jewelry, old books, pottery, and various odds and ends went on for what seemed like miles.

Krish cleared his throat and didn't pull his gaze from

Saraya while he spoke. "We have a lead. While combing through Lord Ritvik's personal papers, we found a returned letter from his father to an old seer named Neela. No one has heard from him in decades, nor has a clue as to where to find him. I took a picture of the letter." He reached into his pocket and pulled out his phone. After a few swipes, he passed it to Reggie. "See what you make of this."

Nettie scooted closer to Reggie to view the screen. Through her sweater, his body burned hot and his pulse raced. As they bent their heads over the phone, she stretched to whisper in his ear. "You're doing great staying in control. Just a little bit longer."

He nodded, and they began to read. The two lines Krish had highlighted stood out:

> To save the land of fire and dust, you must seek out a branch from a rare tree, deep in the forest of enchantment. Let the birds guide you.

"A branch?" Reggie read the highlighted lines again. "So you think he could be referring to the wand, and Neela has it?"

"Or he knows who does." Krish supplied. He leaned forward and rested his forearms on his knees, but didn't let go of Saraya's hand. "We think Lord Ritvik purposely advised Saraya's parents to a match with Ardu Almaar, but we don't know why."

Nettie slid her hand out of his and glanced at Reggie with a big grin on her face. He handed her the phone, bewildered. How could she smile when they were no closer to a solution? The riddle was the writing of a crazy old lunatic.

She stood up and began pacing the length of the tiny room, back and forth between the sofa and the coffee table. "There's so much more here. This one—'when the dark prince chooses the lotus blossom, the wand will unlock the phoenix's gifts.' He goes on to say that the *bird of paradise* must facilitate such an exchange. Everything is in place to break the curse! We just need the wand!"

Seven sets of eyes stared at her blankly.

"Don't you get it?" They all shook their heads. "Lord Ritvik mumbled something about a swan. I am a swan from Parajsë, which translates to paradise. I'm the *bird* of *paradise!*"

Saraya gasped, and they all stared at Nettie. Reggie knew she was right; nothing else made any sense.

"We need to track down Neela, or the wand, or both." Krish turned to Denpo. "We need to go to the Enchanted Wood. Do whatever you need to do to get us there. As quickly as possible."

The guard stepped back into the corner of the room and pressed his hand to a screen on the wall. After the laser scan, and panel swung open revealing a keyboard and trio of monitors. Reggie stared in awe as his fingers flew furiously across the keyboard.

Saraya addressed her guard. "Pemela, how are we doing on time?"

"Two minutes longer, your Royal Highness."

Saraya explained. "We want to give all appearances that this is a normal tour, one reserved only for our most esteemed visitors, of course, such as the betrothed of the Princess Royal." Reggie stared at her; his mouth agape. Her lips twitched. "It's quite a normal thing to want to appraise a kingdom's resources before making the union official, I'm sure."

Reggie didn't understand how she could speak so easily. Was it for the benefit of Krish, similar to how Nettie was doing all she could to convince him everything would work out?

"Time," Pemela announced, then addressed her partner. "Den, how much longer do you need?"

Denpo's fingers stilled at the keyboard. "Less than a minute." They all watched as he launched into a final typing spree and then closed up the unit. "Reconvene at noon tomorrow at the helipad. Best way for Her Royal Highness's betrothed to tour the island, no?"

Reggie wished they'd stop calling him that. He didn't want to be Saraya's betrothed, and he knew the farce was helpful to their cause, but it bothered him. And if it bothered him, surely it bothered Nettie to some degree. Didn't it?

PROMPTLY AT NOON, Nettie, Reggie, Saraya, Krish, and their guards exited the palace and crossed the snow-covered gardens to the helipad. Two birds, as they were called, awaited them.

The irony wasn't lost on Nettie. Poor Reggie was going to burst if he couldn't shift sooner rather than later, though. She'd never been prouder of him. He was doing an exemplary job of controlling his emotions, and by extension, his shifting.

The guards conferenced briefly with the pilots, and then to Nettie's surprise, the pilots climbed into a waiting Humvee just to the side of the double helipad. Elie and Telavi saluted them as the Humvee drove away.

"You fly, too?" Nettie asked Elie incredulously as she processed what was happening.

The guard smiled. "At our rank, we all do, your Royal Highness. It's a survival skill anyone guarding the royal family must have."

Elie settled in the pilot's seat as Telavi assisted Nettie into the helicopter. Once the four of them were seated, Telavi turned to face her and Reggie. "We'll fly to the last known location Neela was reportedly spotted at, over thirty years ago. Our intelligence team in the south shore's wetlands communities have secured it and are awaiting us."

Nettie kept her eyes on Reggie as he relaxed into his seat. She could feel deep within her his inability to shake the feeling of hopelessness. Finding an old guy in a jungle community after thirty years seemed impossible, even to her.

It was too loud to talk, even with the headphones on, so she just held his hand and stared out the window. Below, the mountains gave way to patchwork farms and then beaches. As they flew along the coast, Reggie's hand heated to almost scorching as he fought his body's primal need to transform.

Just when she felt she might sustain a serious burn; the helicopter began its descent toward a clearing in the palms. Nettie gently pulled her hand from Reggie's grip and pressed it to the cool glass beside her. The steam from her skin created a fog that fanned out over the glass, distorting the images on the other side.

The other copter landed first, in the northeast corner of the clearing near the narrow river that ribboned through it. Elie and Telavi set their aircraft down as close to the other as safety allowed.

A group of uniformed Pundarikan soldiers surrounded them. While the guards spoke to the captain of the local force, Nettie caught Saraya's eyes. Within their dark, gold-flecked depths, was raw determination. A kindred feeling passed between them, and Nettie was reassured that she wasn't the only one that would fight this injustice to the end.

After the obligatory ceremonial greeting, the soldiers led the group over a small bridge to the other side of the river, where a permanent structure sat on the bank. The concrete command center was partially camouflaged with dark green paint and covered in natural vegetation.

Nettie clung to Reggie's arm as they followed Krish and Saraya inside to a plushly-furnished room not unlike the one in the archives bunker. On the far wall, a media screen was pulled down as if waiting for a presentation.

Krish remained standing with the guards as the princesses and Reggie sat on the sofas. The younger prince was calm. The only indication of his agitation was the occasional twitch of the muscle at his left temple.

"Your Royal Highnesses." One of the two men at the wall's computer bowed and gestured to his colleague once the heavy door had been secured. He flashed his identification to Krish and addressed the others. "My code name is Sekrit. I am one of the agents assigned to this region." Sekrit nodded to the other man.

"Seely Brennington. It's delightful to meet you in person, Your Royal Highnesses. We at the Brennington Intelligence Agency are humbled and honored to be in your service. Sekrit and I have unearthed two leads and have agents pursuing both." He held up an electronic tablet and scrolled. "Neela of Colaba Rock, was last seen thirty years ago about a mile from here in a cave. My men have completed a forensic search of the cave and discovered an intricate tunnel system both above and below ground, as well as some relics, carvings on the wall, and a pile of bones, which we are currently analyzing." At Saraya's soft gasp, he explained further. "Animal bones, belonging to small mammals and large birds. However, we're sending them to the nearest lab for analysis in case there are human bones mixed in."

Sekrit typed onto the keyboard and a map lit up the screen. "The cave is here." He drew a circle on the tablet with his finger which then appeared before them. "Over here," he drew an *X* about a half mile from the cave, "is where Parvatidurga lives, the oldest woman in these parts. She doesn't appear to be completely sane, so I recorded what she told us and had it transcribed." The screen changed to reveal a page of text with portions highlighted in yellow. "We aren't sure what this means yet."

PARVATIDURGA: *"Said the little red bird would come for him. 'S why he lived in the cave. Chasing him for years. Had to hide, hide hide! So scared of the little red bird! Little red singing bird! From a faraway land. But she found him. She talked to me, she did. Long time ago. So long time ago. Looking for her friend, the blue bird, she was. Looking for him. I didn't see any blue birds here. She couldn't hurt anyone so I sent her to Neela, I did. Shouldn't have. He never come out of the cave. But red bird found blue bird! Saw them I did."*

SEKRIT: *What did the red bird want with Neela?*

PARVATIDURGA: *(hopping and dancing) They wanted his secrets, of course!*

SEKRIT: *How can you be sure?*

PARVATIDURGA: *Many bad people. Red bird told me Neela would only be safe at her place.*

SEKRIT: *Did red bird say where she was from?*

PARVATIDURGA: *No, but the fine carriage had horses that fly!*

SEKRIT: *There was a carriage? Was there anyone in the carriage?*

PARVATIDURGA: *(Shrugs)*

SEKRIT: *Were there any markings on the carriage?*

PARVATIDURGA: *A shield and a crown and two pretty white horses and [unintelligible]*

Nettie cried out. "It's Once Upon Academy!"

R eggie stared in disbelief. Was it possible Neela had been at Once Upon Academy for three decades? And if so, where would they find him?

"Do you have a picture of him?" he asked.

The screen changed. Reggie, Nettie, and Krish peered at the man. Saraya stood and tapped her foot. "Surely you've seen him before?"

Reggie shook his head slowly. "I've been there for almost five years. I've never seen anyone who looked like this."

"Maybe he's living in the Enchanted Wood, or locked up in the dungeon?" Nettie suggested.

"The Headmistress would know." Reggie held up his phone and took a picture of the screen. "She has to."

Krish stood up. "Then let's get back there. Tonight."

BACK AT ONCE UPON ACADEMY, Nettie, Reggie, Krish, and Saraya waited to be admitted into the Headmistress's office.

Nettie placed a protective hand over her tote, where she kept the book that had started them on their quest. The Headmistress *had* to know.

"Ahem." A soft voice commanded their attention. Nettie turned to find Ms. Fay standing a few feet away. "I see Saraya got past the security spell again. Young lady, princess and legacy or not, you aren't a student here. Care to explain?"

"I—we—" Saraya's widened eyes pleaded with Ms. Fay.

Krish took over. "We need to speak with the Headmistress. It's an urgent matter of national security for Ardu Almaar and Pundarika."

Ms. Fay's lips twitched. "I can assure you it's not, or I wouldn't be finding out from you four." Her voice softened. "The Headmistress is currently out of realm. What can I help you with, dears?"

Nettie's heart twinged as Reggie's face fell. He exchanged a glance with Krish, who nodded for him to speak "We're looking for someone. And we think Headmistress might know where to find him."

Ms. Fay waved her wand at the door. It sparkled briefly

as the mechanism unlocked. "I guess we'd better go in then."

After sealing the door behind them, Ms. Fay faced the students. "Do explain."

As they took turns telling the story, Nettie watched Ms. Fay for reactions. She kept her face neutral the entire time, like a practiced monarch.

This wasn't going to be easy.

"And you think this Neela character is here? At OUA? I assure you, if he is, it's likely classified."

"So you can't tell us?" Saraya wailed. "Please, Ms. Fay. All of our futures depend on it."

Ms. Fay's expression hardened. "No. That's where you're wrong, young princess. Your future depends on *you*, and the choices *you* make."

Reggie let out an exasperated breath. "We can't make a choice if we don't have the information we need!"

"Oh, but you do, Reggie." She nodded. "Here, take a look." With a flick of her wand, she conjured a long oval in the air in front of them. Inside, a montage of scenes from the last few days played.

"I don't understand," Nettie said. "We know all that. We were there."

Ms. Fay let her wand fall to her side and the images faded away. "Then maybe you ought to look at them with another perspective. A bird's eye view, say."

"Are you saying we should shift?" Reggie asked. Nettie held her breath. Could it be that simple?

"Is he camped in the Enchanted Woods? Could we spot him from the air?" Nettie spoke fast as her heart rate sped up.

Ms. Fay's face was again unreadable. "What I'm saying is, *you* are capable of solving this problem yourselves. Now get to it, and keep mind tomorrow's Monday. Don't miss classes," she warned.

Back in the hall, Nettie took Reggie's hand.

"The tower," they said at the same time.

TEN

Reggie almost laughed when he opened the door to the top level of the astronomy tower. The interior had been transformed in their absence. The equipment was gone, and in its place was a large stone table. On each side of it, heavy velvet curtains in OUA's shade of purple cordoned off two private areas, one labeled "Princes" and the other "Princesses."

"Well, at least we know she meant for us to come here," Nettie joked, tightening her grip on his hand.

"Let's go over the plan before you shift." Krish was all business. Reggie was glad he was taking charge. His brother would make a fine king if he got the chance.

They had to fix this. *He* had to fix this, and right the wrong and break the curse. "Nettie and I will fly over the forest, looking for structures or signs of human activity. You two will head into the woods with the evidence and our clothes and wait for us at the abandoned dwarves' house. We'll meet up there when we find something, or at sunrise, whichever comes first."

"Good luck, brother. We'll be waiting." For a second, Krish's voice wavered. Reggie swallowed a lump in his throat. His brother was being tough because he had to be, but it didn't mean he didn't need love. Reggie wondered if Saraya was the only one who'd ever given it to him unconditionally.

"Thank you." Before he had time to decide against it, Reggie took the hand Krish offered.

Instead of shaking it, he clasped it firmly and pulled his brother to him for a brief hug.

Krish stiffened, then patted him on the back awkwardly before backing away. "Yes, er. Just find the man."

Ten minutes later, Reggie and Nettie, in their avian forms, perched on the stone sill. *The swan and the phoenix.* His nerves tingled in anticipation.

Their gazes met and he nodded. Nettie raised her wings and glided off the sill. He followed, leaving a trail of sparks behind him. Side by side, they flew over above the trees, over the lake, past the Headmistress's mansion, and to the Enchanted Woods.

Reggie hadn't spent any time during his four-and-a-half years in the Enchanted Woods area of OUA's grounds, having only utilized it to travel among the realms and to cut through occasionally when he and his friends wanted to go to the beach, which laid on the other side. Beneath the canopy lived ominous creatures that he preferred not to encounter. Last semester's ogre incident had only served to reaffirm Reggie's opinions on the territory.

After hours of searching, Reggie flew to the meeting point. As he descended, he saw Nettie through the window with Saraya and Krish. He used his beak to peck lightly on the glass and glided down to the doorway.

From a nearby tree, a trilling caught his attention. He turned to find Azure, the Headmistress's bird, perched on a branch above him.

Azure, like his name, was a blue bird of nondescript breed.

A blue bird!

Could birds talk to each other? He and Nettie could read each other's minds, but he'd never tried to communicate with a non-shifting bird before. What if Azure knew of the bird they sought?

He closed his eyes and concentrated. Behind him, the door opened and he caught a whiff of Nettie's vanilla scent. *Clear your thoughts.*

Opening his eyes, he met the little bird's gaze. *Do you know of a blue bird that knows a man named Neela?*

Azure nodded and fluttered to the ground. *I think we'd better go inside.*

Nettie ushered Reggie inside the cottage and gestured to the curtain rigged up in the corner. "You can change there. Why, hello, Azure!"

Reggie shifted and dressed quickly. As he came around the corner, Azure passed him. He shot the bird a quizzical glance and crossed the planked floor to sit at the table with the others.

"From your expression, I take it the search was a failure as well?" Krish asked sharply. "Probably. Azure implied he knew something, but—"

"Azure knows everything!" A man's high-pitched voice caused them all to jerk their heads in the direction of the curtain. Two sets of fingers appeared on either side of the fabric, and rolled inward, forming around a body. It turned, revealing a small, elderly man's head within the folds.

Saraya gasped. "Who are you? Why are you here?"

"It has been prophesized, of course," the man said. "I am Neela, and quite pleased to finally make your acquaintances, Princes Reginald and Krish. And yours, Princesses Antionette and Saraya. We've much to discuss."

NETTIE STARED open-mouthed at the old man. Azure was Neela? Had the Headmistress known? "Did the Headmistress—"

"Send me to find you, yes, yes," the old man sputtered. He wobbled to the table. Reggie rose from his chair. "Please, have a seat."

"Can I get you water? Tea?" Saraya asked.

"Tea would be lovely, thank you." Neela gripped the table as he lowered himself into the chair. "It's been a long time since I've shifted. You must forgive my awkwardness."

"Of course." Nettie studied the old man. "So, how long have you been at Once Upon Academy? Why are you in disguise? And how can you help us?"

Neela chuckled and glanced at Reggie. "She gets straight to the point. I like that." He smiled. "Long ago, Ardu Almaar was cursed."

"We know that, old man!" Krish shouted. "How can we fix this?" "Can I transfer my shifting to Krish?" Reggie swallowed. "Reggie!" Nettie gasped. "Give up flying?"

He took a deep breath. "You are more important than flying." He looked around the table. "You all are."

From the looks on their faces, Krish and Saraya were as stunned as she was. "Neela, can we do that? Will it help?"

"There is no way to break the curse, or transfer powers, unfortunately. But we *can* split it with the right tool. While I was a student here, my friend and I discovered a way to use gold to split curses. We were trying to break them of course, but some require the knowledge of unknown magic that students like us did not have access to."

"How does it work?" Reggie asked.

The man smiled. "You simply ask the tool to manifest what you want."

"That sounds too easy," Krish said. "What's the catch?"

"Only that all parts must be accounted for."

Nettie ruminated over the Neela's information. "So, in this case, which I assume you know all about?" Neela nodded. "We could split the curse. So Reggie could remain a phoenix and Krish could rule?"

"Normally, yes. But there is something you are all overlooking. The curse only applies to *legitimate* heirs." He twisted to point a finger to Reggie, standing beside him. "You, lad, are not legitimate. If you were to rule, your kingdom will meet its end."

"But I'm not a phoenix." Krish slammed his hands on the table and stood up. His eyes flashed at Neela. "How do we fix this?"

Neela shrugged. "The golden wand, of course. How else?"

"Why wouldn't the Headmistress just tell us?" Reggie asked. "Why put us through this and risk Ardu Almaar, and Pundarika, by proxy?"

"She had to be sure of your true motives. *All* of your true motives. Nettie had transformed granite into gold. Reggie has offered to give up his gift of flying. Krish has proven his aptitude for leadership, and Saraya's heart for the people of Ardu Almaar, as well as her own homeland, has been revealed to be true and constant. I believe your quest has proven you all worthy of choosing your own destiny. Which is exactly what is needed for the wand to work. You need only to complete the final step, my bird of paradise. A happy accident, no?"

Nettie raised a brow at the phrase, which Professor Peabody also used. "Most definitely.

"But where is the wand?"

Neela lifted his hand and rotated his wrist. "Right here." Out of thin air, a golden stick materialized in his grip. "All you have to do is tell it to do what you want it to do."

R eggie stood beside Krish and Saraya against the far wall in the alchemy lab. Across the room, Nettie and Professor Peabody bent over a collection of flasks and tubes. On the table, turned to the last page, was Ritvik's book.

Neela, in avian form, perched on Nettie's shoulder supervising the activity. Before transforming, he'd told her the recipe had been written in code into the summary of the thesis. It hadn't taken her long to decipher the hidden message.

Professor Peabody whooped, whirling in a circle and clapping his hands. "My girl, you did it!"

Saraya squealed and through her arms around Krish. Reggie grinned at them and closed the distance between him and Nettie, who's self-satisfied half-smile confirmed the professor's claim.

Reggie stopped just short of the table. "Uh...is it safe to get closer?"

Nettie laughed and nodded, reaching for his hand. "Come here and see." She gave a gentle tug and he stepped into place beside her. "Since we already had the magical gold I created, the next part was easy. Each end of the wand needed to be infused with new magic by my creation. Each end of the wand is changed with opposite magnetic forces that will repel each other. So, with the right incantation, it will do exactly as you command. You simply have to hold it and speak the words. At the last word, Krish will also take hold and the power absorbed from you will repel onto him."

"And that's it?" Reggie swallowed. "Seems pretty fast. When—" he turned to face his brother. "When shall we do this?"

Krish frowned. "I'm ready now. Are you having second thoughts?"

"No, just..." He turned back to Nettie. "How about one last flight together, before I lose my gift?"

"Reg." Nettie cupped his cheek with her palm. "It doesn't have to be right now." She looked past him to Krish and Saraya. "Can't we wait? Give him more time?"

"No," Reggie said. He didn't know how much longer the king had. He covered her palm with his. "I'm ready. I just want one more flight."

"Then get to it, lovebirds! Oooh-hooo! Pun intended!" Professor Peabody's gleeful laugh broke the tension. "I'll leave you kids to do the cleanup. Antoinette, you know how to find me if you need further assistance. Might I suggest completing your project in the Headmistress's office, in case you run into trouble or lose a finger or something?"

"Yes, Professor," Nettie chuckled. "We've got this."

Two hours later, and after an exhilarating flight soaring over campus and all the grounds, Nettie and Reggie met Krish and Saraya in the Headmistress's office.

Azure—Neela—perched on her desk.

"Are you ready, Reggie?" Her soft, singsong voice didn't help to ease his nervousness.

"I am. Be ready at the last word, brother." He took a deep breath and closed his eyes,

clutching the wand with all his strength. "Paradise gold, phoenix twofold, transfer my gift to the dark prince's hold."

As Krish's hand closed around the wand, a golden haze radiated from it, traveling up their arms and covering their bodies from head to toe. Reggie felt a suction, but no pain, and then a vibration that knocked him off balance. He struggled to keep his hold on the stone as he fell with Krish to the floor.

The haze lifted. "Did it work?" Krish asked. He lay on his back, eyes closed.

"Let's see. Sit up, dear," the Headmistress commanded. "Now take your shirts off." Reggie and Krish stared at her.

"Don't get your feathers ruffled, boys. It's simply to see if the birthmark transferred." She shook her head. "Goodness."

He looked at his brother and they shrugged. Together, they lifted their shirts up and over their heads.

A collective gasp filled the room. "What is it?" Krish asked.

Saraya could only stare. Reggie looked at Nettie.

"You both have the birthmark! Headmistress, does this mean what I think it means?"

"It certainly does. Two phoenixes. Congratulations, dears!"

LATER THAT NIGHT, after a whirlwind ride in one of the Academy's magical carriages, the foursome stood before the king and queen of Ardu Almaar. Nettie stole a glance at Reggie and Krish, dressed regally in the country's colors of burgundy, plum, and gold. Saraya had donned a formal sari in matching colors. Each wore gold-trimmed purple sashes and crowns.

Nettie stood tall in her purple gown while Reggie and Krish shared what they'd learned, aware that her chosen ensemble projected an image of solidarity and unity.

Off to the side, Reggie's half-siblings, also dressed in their finest, watched with curiosity.

The king gave a final weary nod and leaned back in his throne. "And you are certain that the birthright belongs to Krish? My son, have you transformed yet?"

"No, Father. If I'm to follow your and Reggie's precedent, I don't expect to for several more years."

"I don't know if—my health..." The king sighed. "I'm fading, my sons. As my father before me did. I don't know if it's part of the curse or genetics. I pray it's neither, and caused by a lifetime of overindulgence." He gave a weak smile. "What I am sure of, is that this kingdom will be in good hands, with both of you here. Two phoenixes! Who'd have ever thought!" He chuckled as he leaned on the chair's arms to assist him in standing.

"Thank you, Father." Krish said. Nettie couldn't see his face, but he almost sounded...happy.

More than anything, Nettie wanted to jump up and down with joy. They'd done it! She knew the coming years may be difficult, but she was confident that if they all worked together, there was no problem they couldn't solve.

CHAPTER
TWELVE

Later that night, on the palace's highest balcony, Reggie held Nettie close to his side as they looked out upon the kingdom. *Their* kingdom.

Almost. He knew the love between them was the forever kind, but he wanted to make it official.

He angled his face downward to whisper into Nettie's ear. "I love you, Nettie. Thanks for never doubting we'd fix this."

She turned into him and wrapped her arms around his waist. "You'd have done the same if it was the other way around."

He hugged her to him and kissed her forehead. "That's for sure."

The side of her mouth lifted. "Gee, for all that, all I get is a forehead kiss?"

Reggie chuckled. "No. You get everything. If you want

it." He lowered himself to one knee and pulled a ring from his pocket. The sizable ruby caught the moonlight and shimmered with an almost magical fiery glow.

"Oh!" Nettie gasped.

He grinned up at her. "Princess Antoinette of Parajsë, I love you more than anything. I can't imagine a future without you by my side. I want to promise my forever to you. Will you promise your forever to me? "

"It's already yours," Nettie whispered.

Reggie slid the ring on her finger and stood, pulling her back into his arms, knowing that their flame would burn forever.

I hope you enjoyed your visit to Once Upon Academy!

If you loved Nettie and Reggie, please consider leaving a review where you purchased this book, and on Goodreads and BookBub. Reviews are most appreciated and help me decide what to write next!

There's so much more to read and discover!

You can find a map of Once Upon Academy, Nettie's trading card, word searches, a Christmas coloring page, recipes, bonus epilogues, and more on the Freebies page at KerryEvelyn.com! Simply sign up for my newsletter to gain access.

Get more of everything—and me!—when you join my reader group, the Crane's Cove Crew, at Facebook.com/groups/CranesCoveCrew.

Acknowledgments

To the readers—welcome—or welcome back—to OUA! We hope you'll have so much fun you can't wait to return!

Special thanks to Breezy Jones and her team for the concept and invitation to OUA. To all the OUA authors, it's an honor and privilege to be a part of this world with you. Thanks for all the work and imagination you put in to make the Once Upon Academy come to life. I can't wait to see what's next for the students at OUA!

Extra special thanks to Chelsea Fuchs, Alpha Reader since Day 1; Korin Adamites, Beta Reader Extraordinaire; and BookNookNuts for all you do and for loving and supporting your authors.

To Megan Fuentes and Stephanie Harrell, I don't know where to start! It's been so fun hanging out at the Academy with you! Working with you is always a pleasure, and I'm infinitely grateful for your guidance in helping me craft the best story possible. And Megan—this cover—you outdid yourself! I LOVE it!

To Valerie Willis, thank you for always being there for me, for anything, anytime. Since the beginning, you've had such an incredible faith in me, and have supported me in all the things and through all the things. There aren't adequate words to thank you for all the generous time, help, and encouragement you've given me these last five years. I love your heart, and you, so much.

So much gratitude to Andrea Payne, Cindy Montgomery, Valerie Cleveland, and Chris Kridler for their help polishing the most recent edition of this collection—y'all rock! XOXO!

About the Author

Kerry Evelyn is an author and instructor in the Orlando literary community, mentoring student writers and teaching classes for Writer's Atelier, libraries, and professional organizations. Her sweet romance novels feature small towns, a touch of the supernatural, and charming characters pursuing happily-ever-afters. Fueled on faith, Dunkin' iced coffee, and a love for people, including her amazing family, Kerry loves (in ever-changing order) books, boy bands, cats, hockey, sweet drinks, taking selfies, traveling, and the madness of getting the stories in her head onto the page. Find out more and sign up for her newsletter at KerryEvelyn.com/links.

Website: KerryEvelyn.com
Reader Group: Facebook.com/groups/CranesCoveCrew
Email: Kerry@KerryEvelyn.com
Facebook: @KerryEvelynAuthor
Instagram: @KerryEvelynBooks
Twitter:@theKerryEvelyn
TikTok: @KerryEvelynAuthor
Spotify: tinyurl.com/KerryEvelynSpotify
Pinterest: tinyurl.com/KerryEvelynPinterest
Amazon: Amazon.com/Kerry-Evelyn/e/B077LWTYXJ
Goodreads: Goodreads.com/kerryevelynauthor
BookBub: BookBub.com/authors/kerry-evelyn

Books by Kerry Evelyn

Crane's Cove

Love on the Edge

Love on the Rocks

Love on the Beach

Love on the Fly

Love on the Heart

Love on the Brain

A Night at the Inn: A Lizzie Borden Short Story

The Cotton Candy Caper: A Fall Carnival Story

A Night in the Passage: A Crane's Cove Short Story

The Fisherman Nutcracker: A Whimsical Christmas Story

A Night in the Cabin: A Crane's Cove Short Story

A Second Shot at Love: A Second Chance Romance Novelette

A Home for Christmas: A Sweet Southern Christmas Story

Cat's Paw Cove

Moon Mist Manor Book 1: Christmas at Moon Mist Manor

Moon Mist Manor Book 2: Love Overrules the Lawyer

Moon Mist Manor Book 3 The Beachcomber's Buccaneer Bounty

Palmer City Voltage

Love on the Ice: A Sweet Small-Town Second Chance Hockey Romance Novelette

Cruising on Ice: A Sweet Small-Town Friends-to Lovers Hockey Romance

Christmas on Ice: A Sweet Small-Town Holiday Hockey Romance

Sparks on the Ice: A Sweet Small-Town Christmas Auction Short Story (Subscriber Bonus)

Melting the Ice: A Sweet Small-Town Late to Love Hockey Romance

Celebration on Ice: A Small-Town Sweet Second Chance Hockey Romance

Crushing on Ice: A Sweet Small-Town Fake Dating Hockey Romance

Once Upon Academy

Birds of a Feather (Prequel)

Bird's Eye View (Once Upon Academy Volume 1)

Phoenix Rising (A Once Upon Academy Duet)

Collections

Crane's Cove Box Set 1

Small-Town Christmas

Crane's Cove Chronicles

Nonfiction

City Nights (How I Met My Other Anthology)

Fenway: A Beacon of Hope (How I Met My Other 2 Anthology)

The Believer's Journal for Everyday Faith

The Advent Experience Keepsake Planner

How to Binge-Write Your Novel

The Brewer Brides — *Coming Soon!*

Keep Me in Mind (Subscriber Bonus)

One Margarita

Born to Fly

Head Over Boots

'Til You Can't

Two Pink Lines

Goodnight Kiss

Make it Sweet

Barn Song

Nobody But You